STONE ARCH BOOKS
a capstone imprint

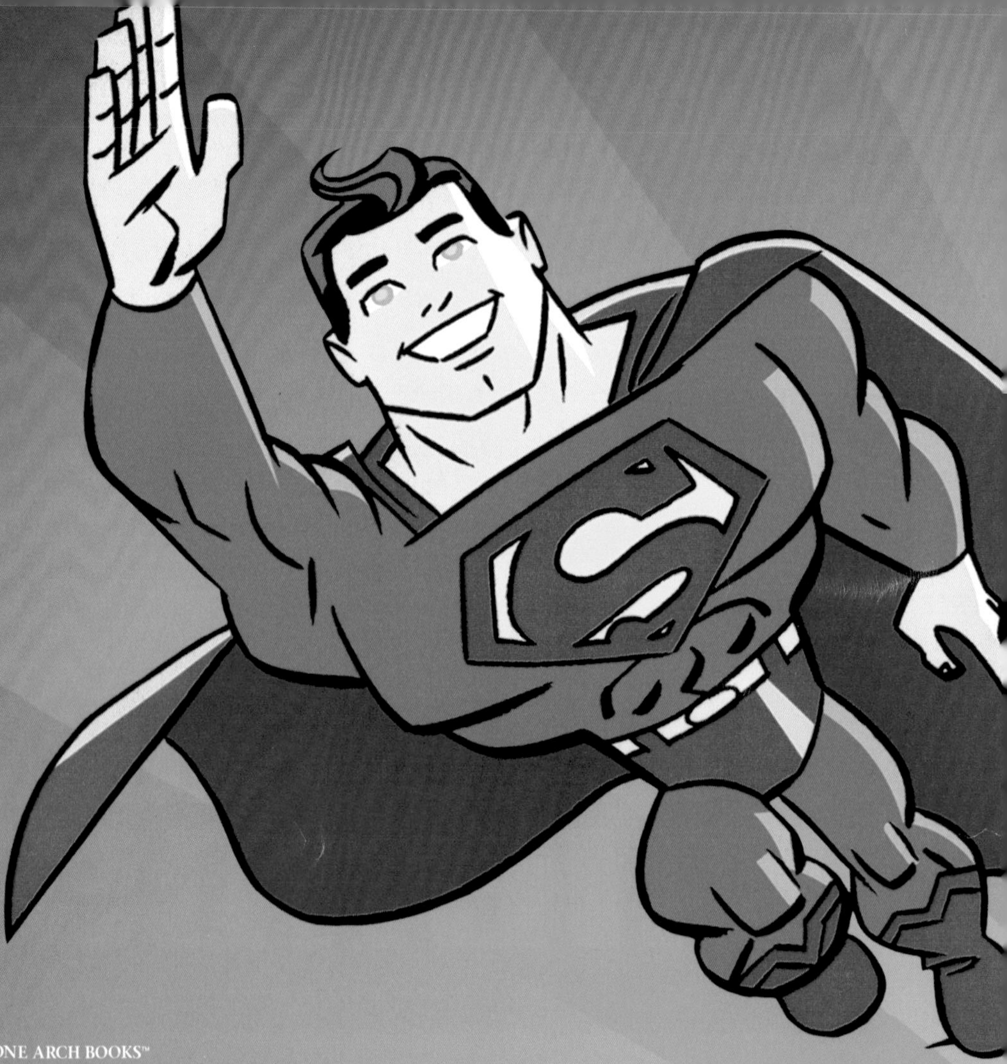

STONE ARCH BOOKS™
Published in 2012
A Capstone Imprint
1710 Roe Crest Drive
North Mankato, MN 56003
www.capstonepub.com

Originally published by DC Comics in
the U.S. in single magazine form as
DC Super Friends #2.

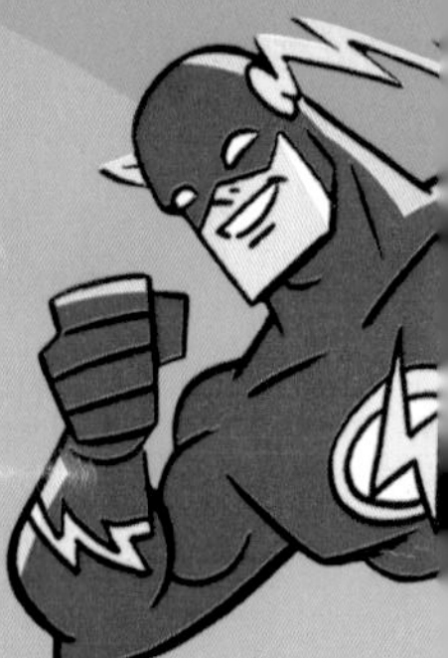

Cataloging-in-Publication Data is available at the
Library of Congress website:
ISBN: 978-1-4342-4542-7 (library binding)

Summary: The World's Greatest Super Heroes are
here to save the day - and be your friends, too! Follow
along as dinosaurs go on a rampage in Metropolis! Will
the Super Friends round up the mighty lizards before
they make too much of a mess?

STONE ARCH BOOKS
Ashley C. Andersen Zantop *Publisher*
Michael Dahl *Editorial Director*
Donald Lemke & Julie Gassman *Editors*
Heather Kindseth *Creative Director*
Brann Garvey *Designer*
Kathy McColley *Production Specialist*

DC COMICS
Rachel Gluckstern *Original U.S. Editor*

Printed in the United States of America
in Brainerd, Minnesota.
122012 007078R

DC Comics
1700 Broadway, New York, NY 10019
A Warner Bros. Entertainment Company

DC★SUPER FRIENDS

DINOSAUR ROUND-UP

Sholly Fisch	....	writer
Joe Staton	....	artist
Horacio Ottolini	....	artist
Heroic Age	....	colorist
Randy Gentile	....	letterer
J. Bone	....	cover artist

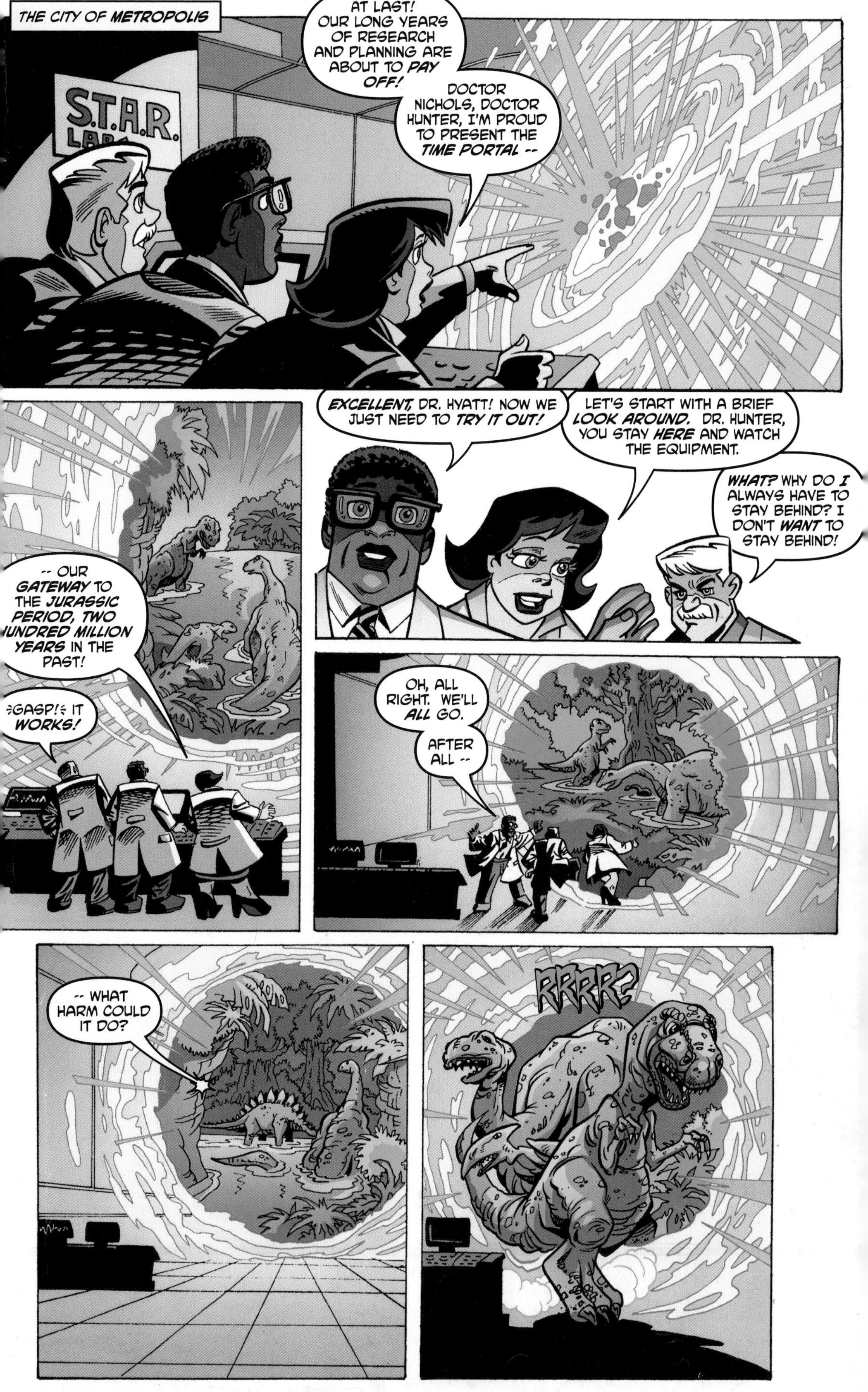
THE CITY OF METROPOLIS
AT LAST! OUR LONG YEARS OF RESEARCH AND PLANNING ARE ABOUT TO PAY OFF!
DOCTOR NICHOLS, DOCTOR HUNTER, I'M PROUD TO PRESENT THE TIME PORTAL --
S.T.A.R.
-- OUR GATEWAY TO THE JURASSIC PERIOD, TWO HUNDRED MILLION YEARS IN THE PAST!
GASP! IT WORKS!
EXCELLENT, DR. HYATT! NOW WE JUST NEED TO TRY IT OUT!
LET'S START WITH A BRIEF LOOK AROUND. DR. HUNTER, YOU STAY HERE AND WATCH THE EQUIPMENT.
WHAT? WHY DO I ALWAYS HAVE TO STAY BEHIND? I DON'T WANT TO STAY BEHIND!
OH, ALL RIGHT. WE'LL ALL GO.
AFTER ALL --
-- WHAT HARM COULD IT DO?
RRRR?

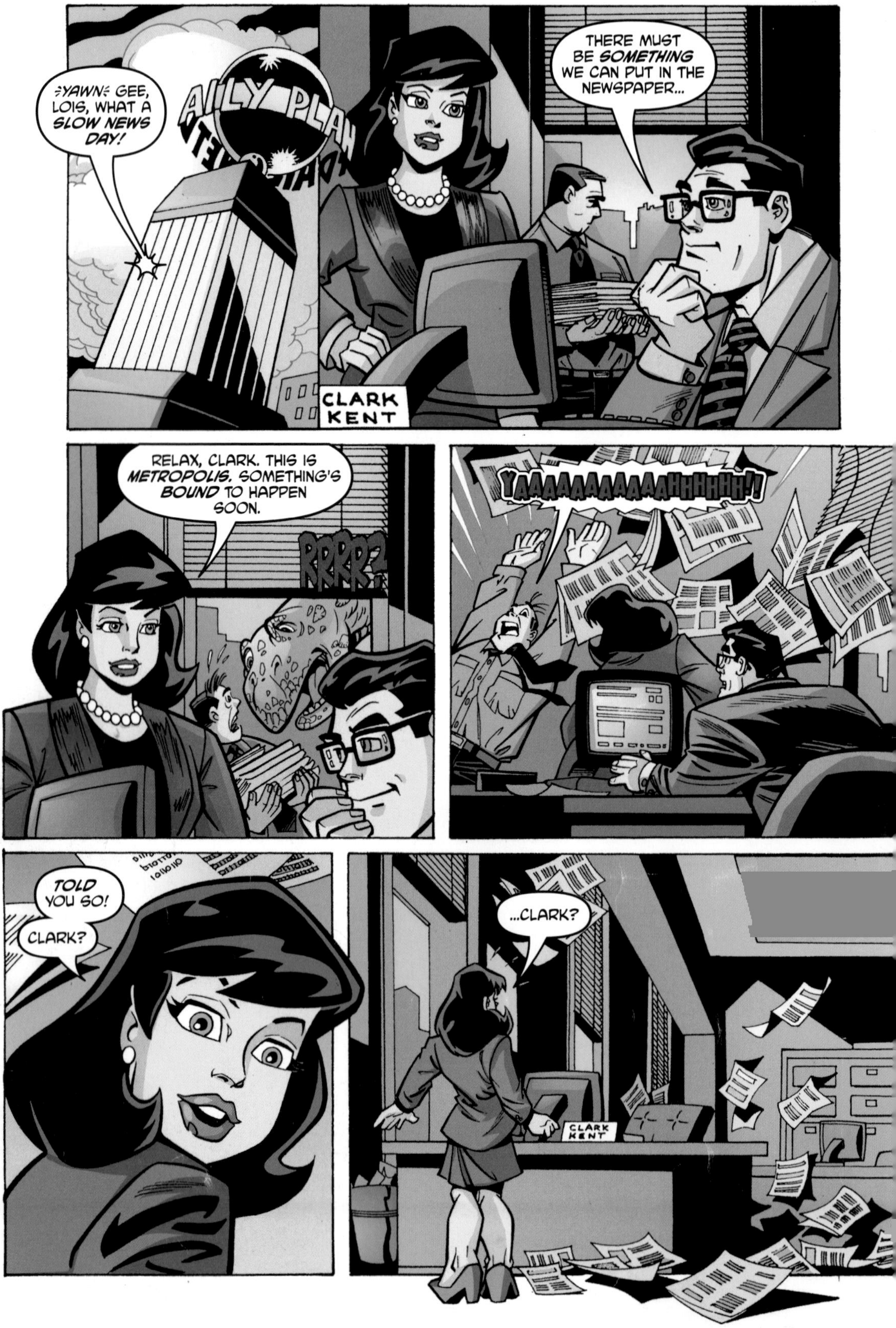

YAWN GEE, LOIS, WHAT A SLOW NEWS DAY!
THERE MUST BE SOMETHING WE CAN PUT IN THE NEWSPAPER...
CLARK KENT
RELAX, CLARK. THIS IS METROPOLIS. SOMETHING'S BOUND TO HAPPEN SOON.
RRRR
YAAAAAAAAAAAHHHHHH!!
TOLD YOU SO!
CLARK?
...CLARK?
CLARK KENT

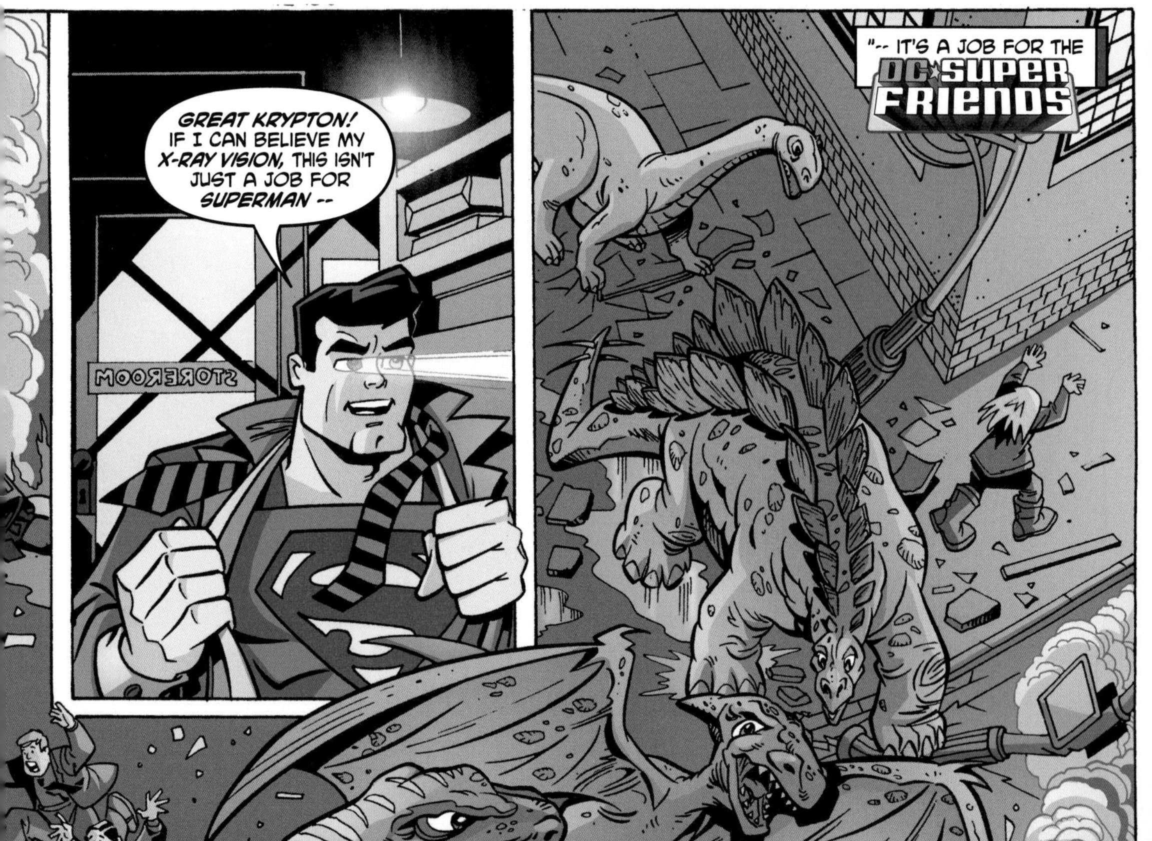
GREAT KRYPTON! IF I CAN BELIEVE MY X-RAY VISION, THIS ISN'T JUST A JOB FOR SUPERMAN --
"-- IT'S A JOB FOR THE
DC SUPER FRIENDS
DINOSAUR ROUND-UP

ROLL CALL!

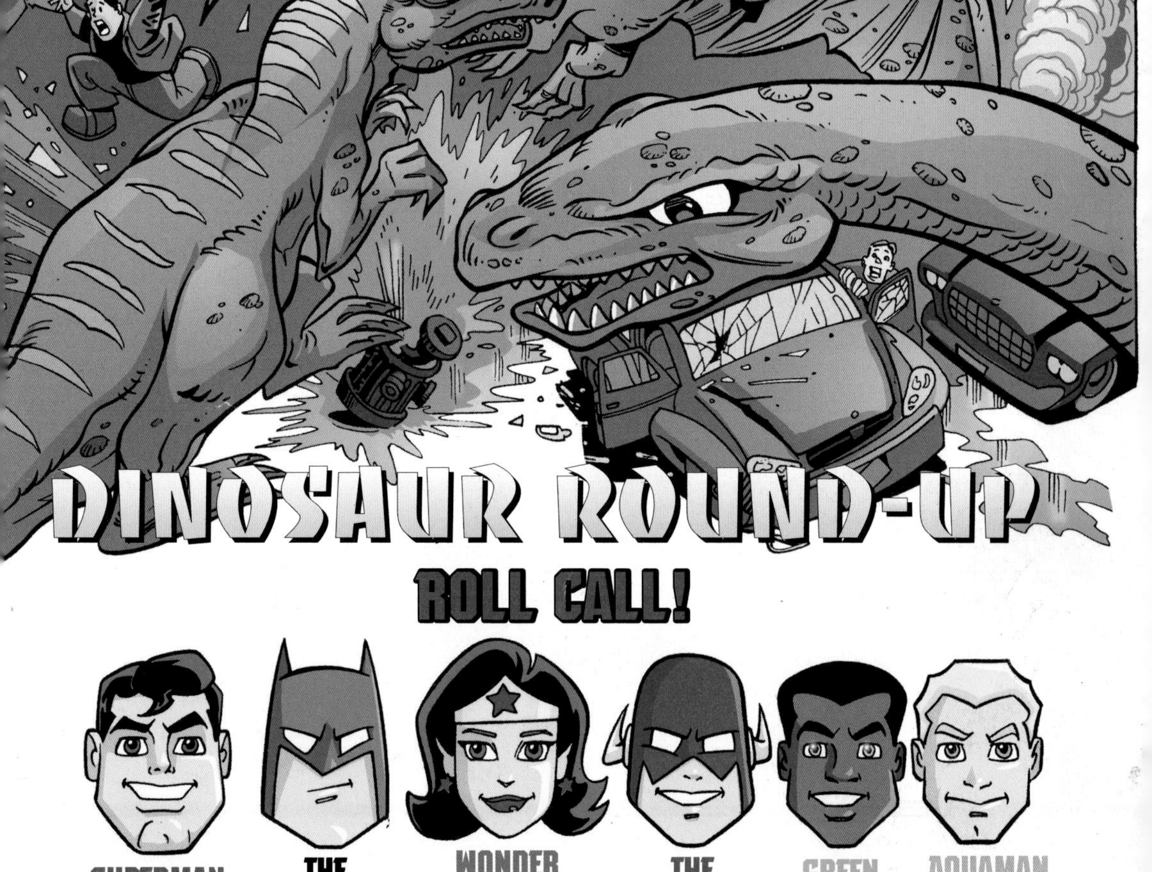

SUPERMAN
MAN OF STEEL

THE BATMAN
DARK KNIGHT DETECTIVE

WONDER WOMAN
AMAZON WARRIOR PRINCESS

THE FLASH
FASTEST MAN ALIVE

GREEN LANTERN
POWER-RINGED GUARDIAN

AQUAMAN
KING OF THE SEA

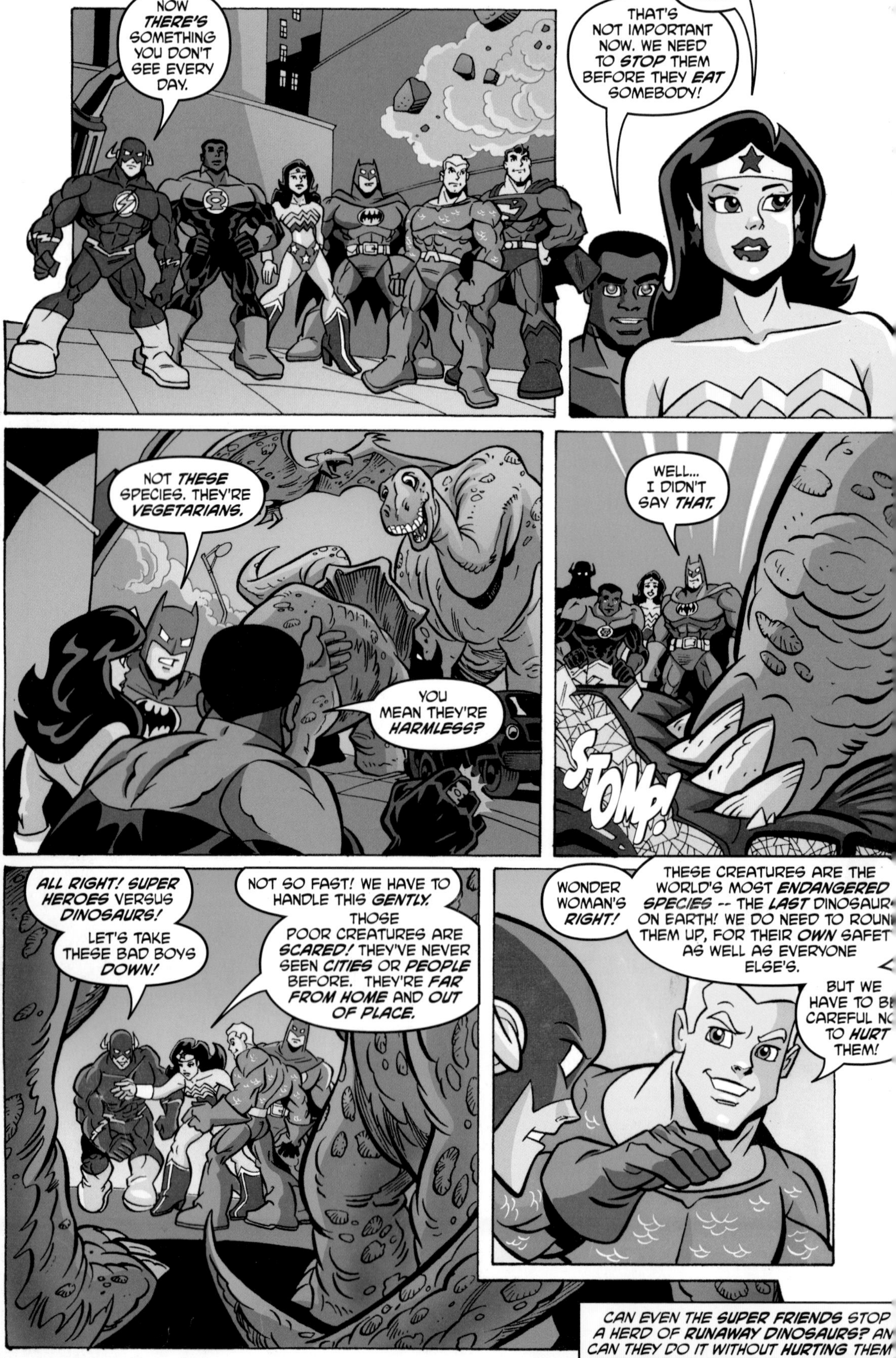
NOW THERE'S SOMETHING YOU DON'T SEE EVERY DAY.
WHERE DID THEY COME FROM?
THAT'S NOT IMPORTANT NOW. WE NEED TO STOP THEM BEFORE THEY EAT SOMEBODY!
NOT THESE SPECIES. THEY'RE VEGETARIANS.
YOU MEAN THEY'RE HARMLESS?
WELL... I DIDN'T SAY THAT.
STOMP!
ALL RIGHT! SUPER HEROES VERSUS DINOSAURS!
LET'S TAKE THESE BAD BOYS DOWN!
NOT SO FAST! WE HAVE TO HANDLE THIS GENTLY.
THOSE POOR CREATURES ARE SCARED! THEY'VE NEVER SEEN CITIES OR PEOPLE BEFORE. THEY'RE FAR FROM HOME AND OUT OF PLACE.
WONDER WOMAN'S RIGHT!
THESE CREATURES ARE THE WORLD'S MOST ENDANGERED SPECIES -- THE LAST DINOSAUR ON EARTH! WE DO NEED TO ROUN THEM UP, FOR THEIR OWN SAFET AS WELL AS EVERYONE ELSE'S.
BUT WE HAVE TO B CAREFUL N TO HURT THEM!
CAN EVEN THE SUPER FRIENDS STOP A HERD OF RUNAWAY DINOSAURS? AN CAN THEY DO IT WITHOUT HURTING THEM KEEP READING TO FIND OUT IN CHAPTER

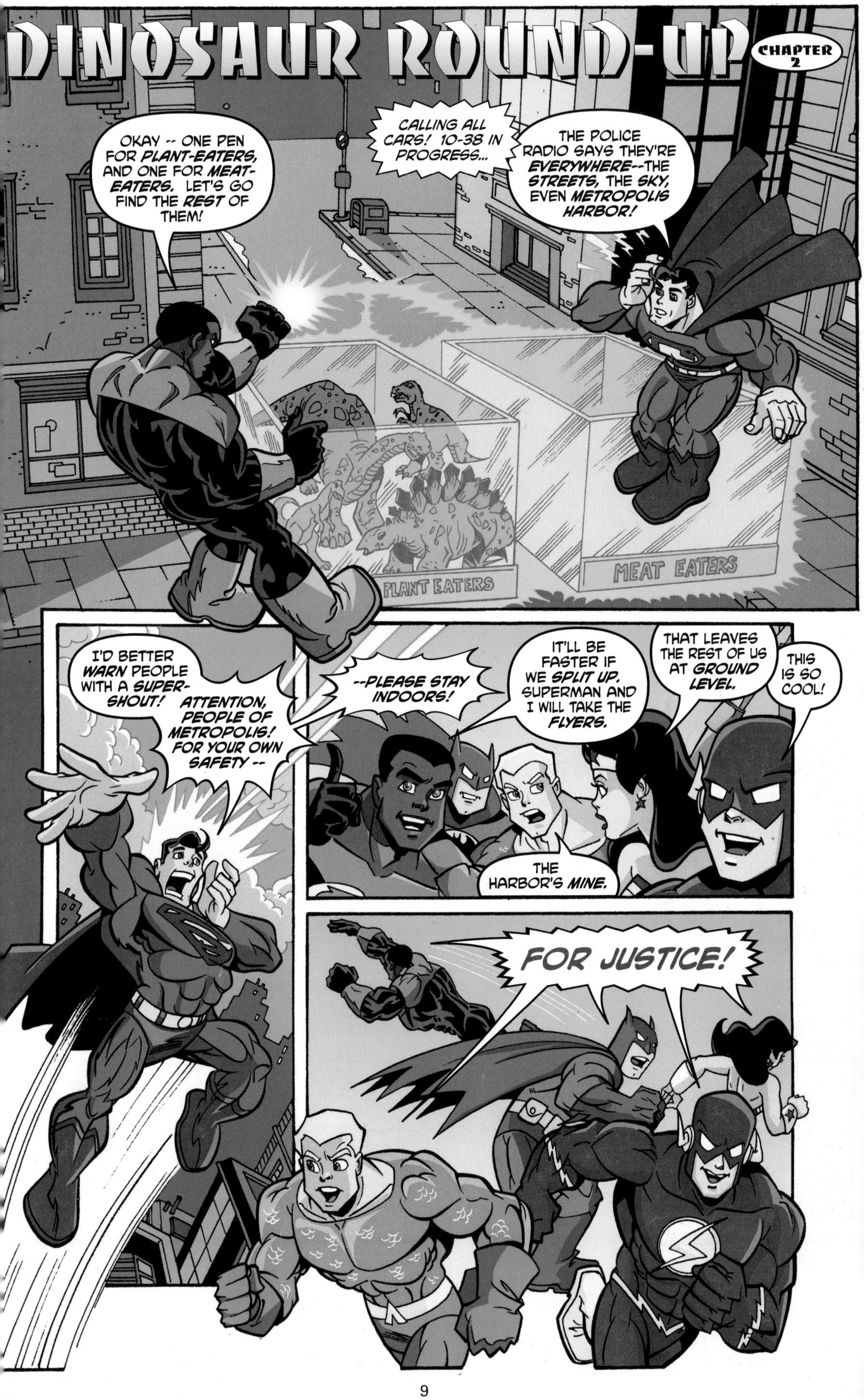
DINOSAUR ROUND-UP
CHAPTER 2
OKAY -- ONE PEN FOR PLANT-EATERS, AND ONE FOR MEAT-EATERS. LET'S GO FIND THE REST OF THEM!
CALLING ALL CARS! 10-38 IN PROGRESS...
THE POLICE RADIO SAYS THEY'RE EVERYWHERE--THE STREETS, THE SKY, EVEN METROPOLIS HARBOR!
PLANT EATERS
MEAT EATERS
I'D BETTER WARN PEOPLE WITH A SUPER-SHOUT!
ATTENTION, PEOPLE OF METROPOLIS! FOR YOUR OWN SAFETY --
--PLEASE STAY INDOORS!
IT'LL BE FASTER IF WE SPLIT UP. SUPERMAN AND I WILL TAKE THE FLYERS.
THAT LEAVES THE REST OF US AT GROUND LEVEL.
THIS IS SO COOL!
THE HARBOR'S MINE.
FOR JUSTICE!

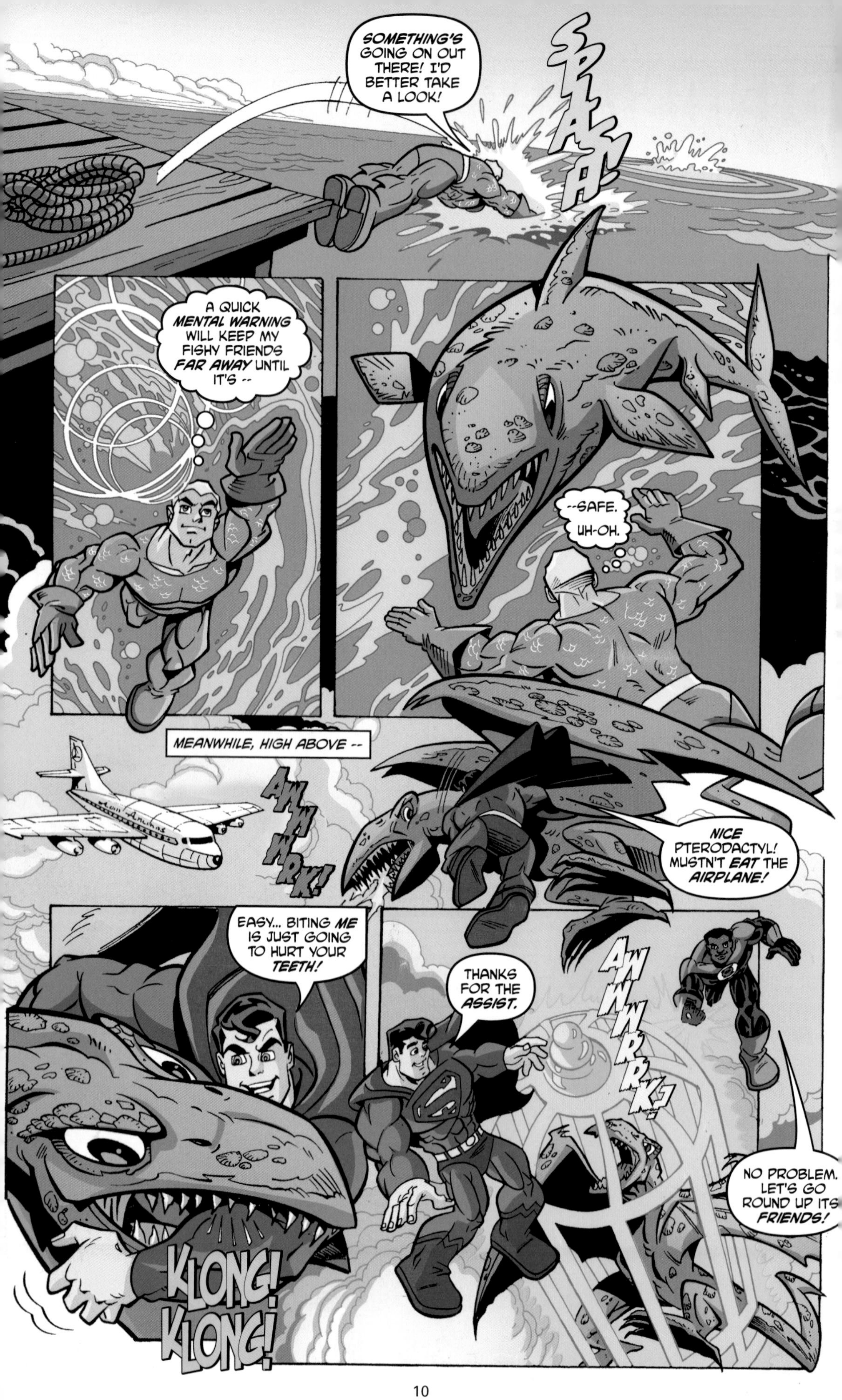

SOMETHING'S GOING ON OUT THERE! I'D BETTER TAKE A LOOK!
SPLASH!
A QUICK MENTAL WARNING WILL KEEP MY FISHY FRIENDS FAR AWAY UNTIL IT'S --
--SAFE. UH-OH.
MEANWHILE, HIGH ABOVE --
AWWWRK!
NICE PTERODACTYL! MUSTN'T EAT THE AIRPLANE!
EASY... BITING ME IS JUST GOING TO HURT YOUR TEETH!
KLONG! KLONG!
THANKS FOR THE ASSIST.
AWWWRK?!
NO PROBLEM. LET'S GO ROUND UP ITS FRIENDS!

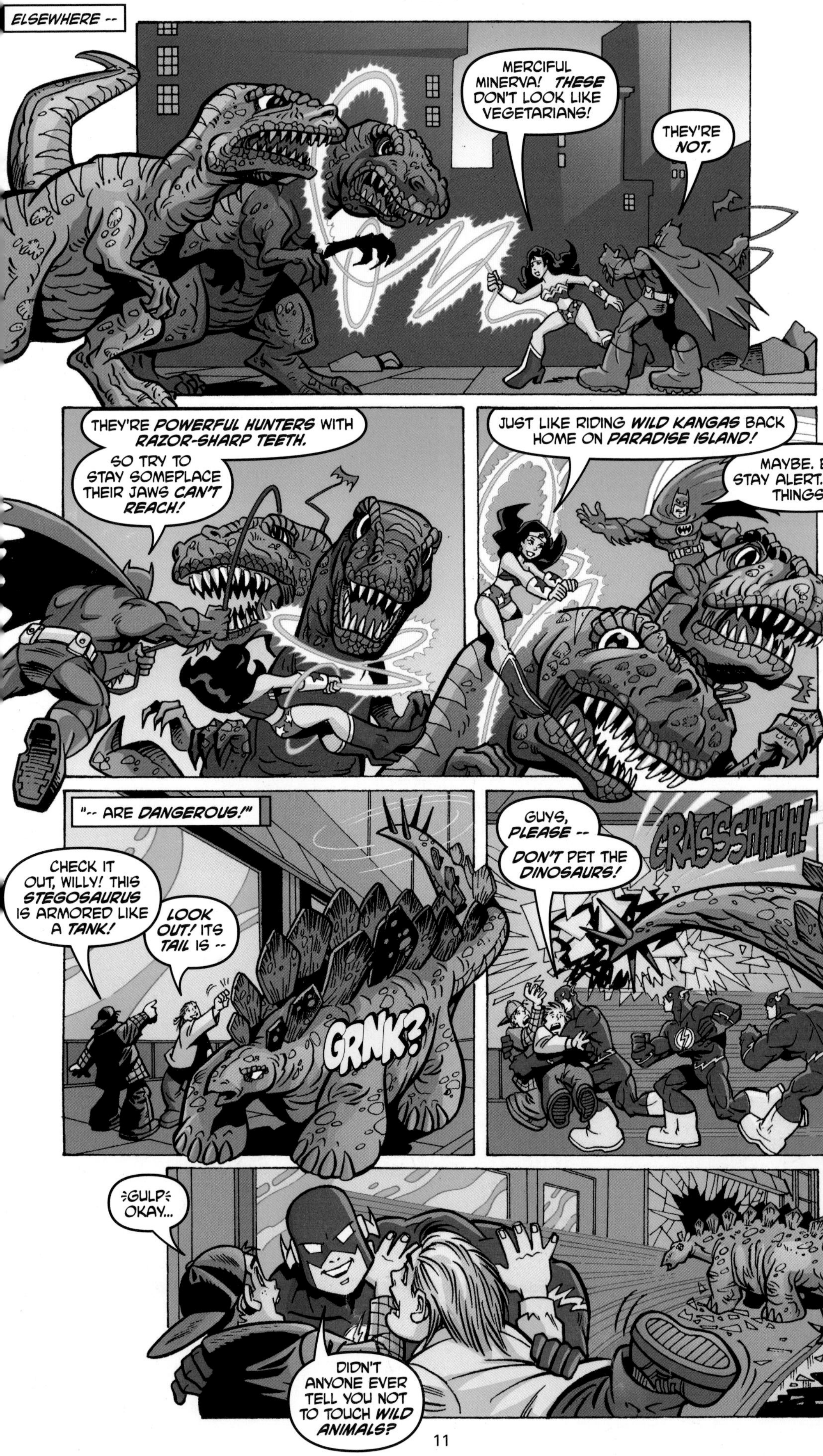
ELSEWHERE --
MERCIFUL MINERVA! THESE DON'T LOOK LIKE VEGETARIANS!
THEY'RE NOT.
THEY'RE POWERFUL HUNTERS WITH RAZOR-SHARP TEETH.
SO TRY TO STAY SOMEPLACE THEIR JAWS CAN'T REACH!
JUST LIKE RIDING WILD KANGAS BACK HOME ON PARADISE ISLAND!
MAYBE. BUT STAY ALERT. THESE THINGS --
"-- ARE DANGEROUS!"
CHECK IT OUT, WILLY! THIS STEGOSAURUS IS ARMORED LIKE A TANK!
LOOK OUT! ITS TAIL IS --
GRNK?
GUYS, PLEASE --
DON'T PET THE DINOSAURS!
CRASSSHHHH!
GULP OKAY...
DIDN'T ANYONE EVER TELL YOU NOT TO TOUCH WILD ANIMALS?

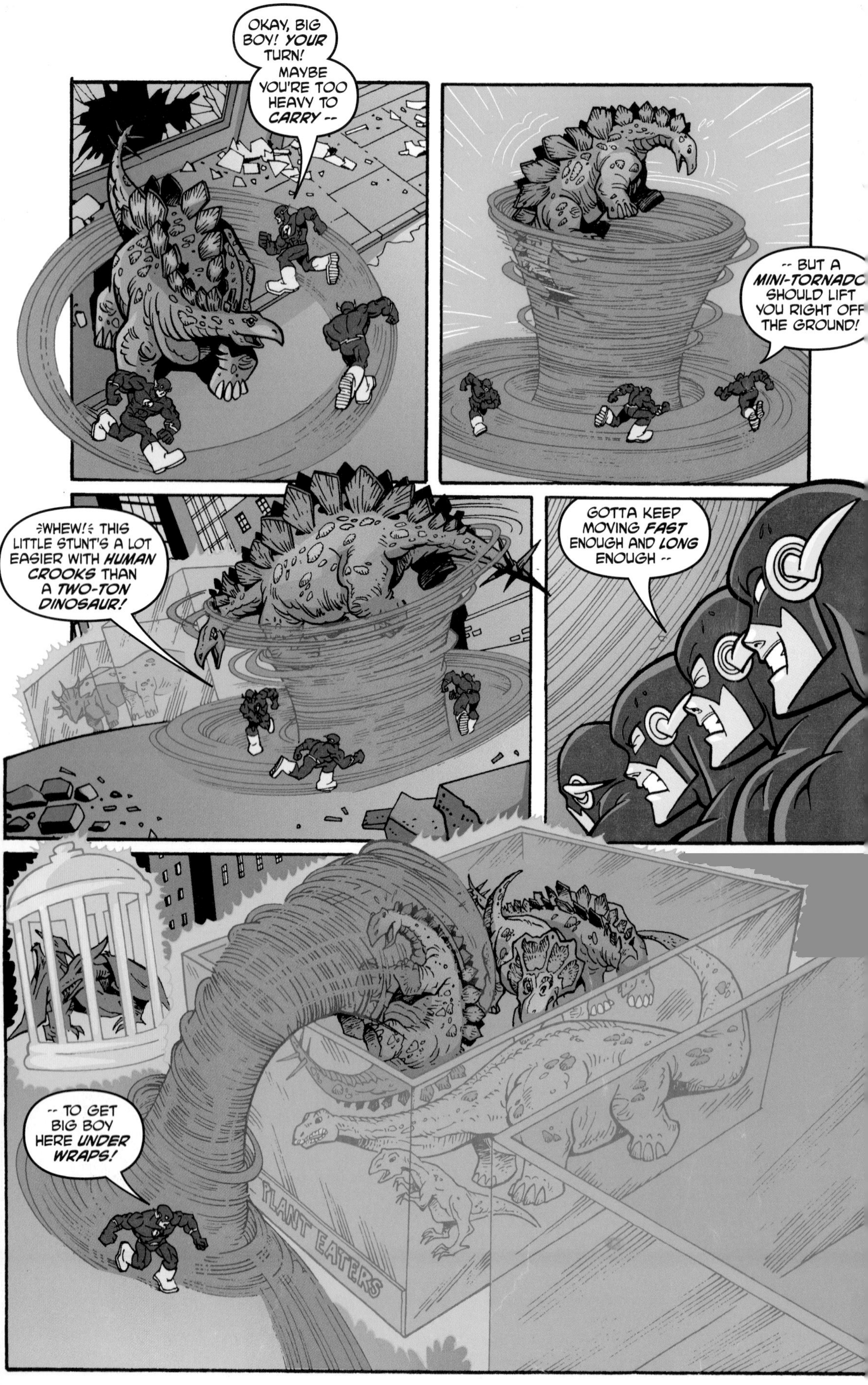
OKAY, BIG BOY! YOUR TURN!
MAYBE YOU'RE TOO HEAVY TO CARRY --
-- BUT A MINI-TORNADO SHOULD LIFT YOU RIGHT OFF THE GROUND!
WHEW! THIS LITTLE STUNT'S A LOT EASIER WITH HUMAN CROOKS THAN A TWO-TON DINOSAUR!
GOTTA KEEP MOVING FAST ENOUGH AND LONG ENOUGH --
-- TO GET BIG BOY HERE UNDER WRAPS!
PLANT EATERS

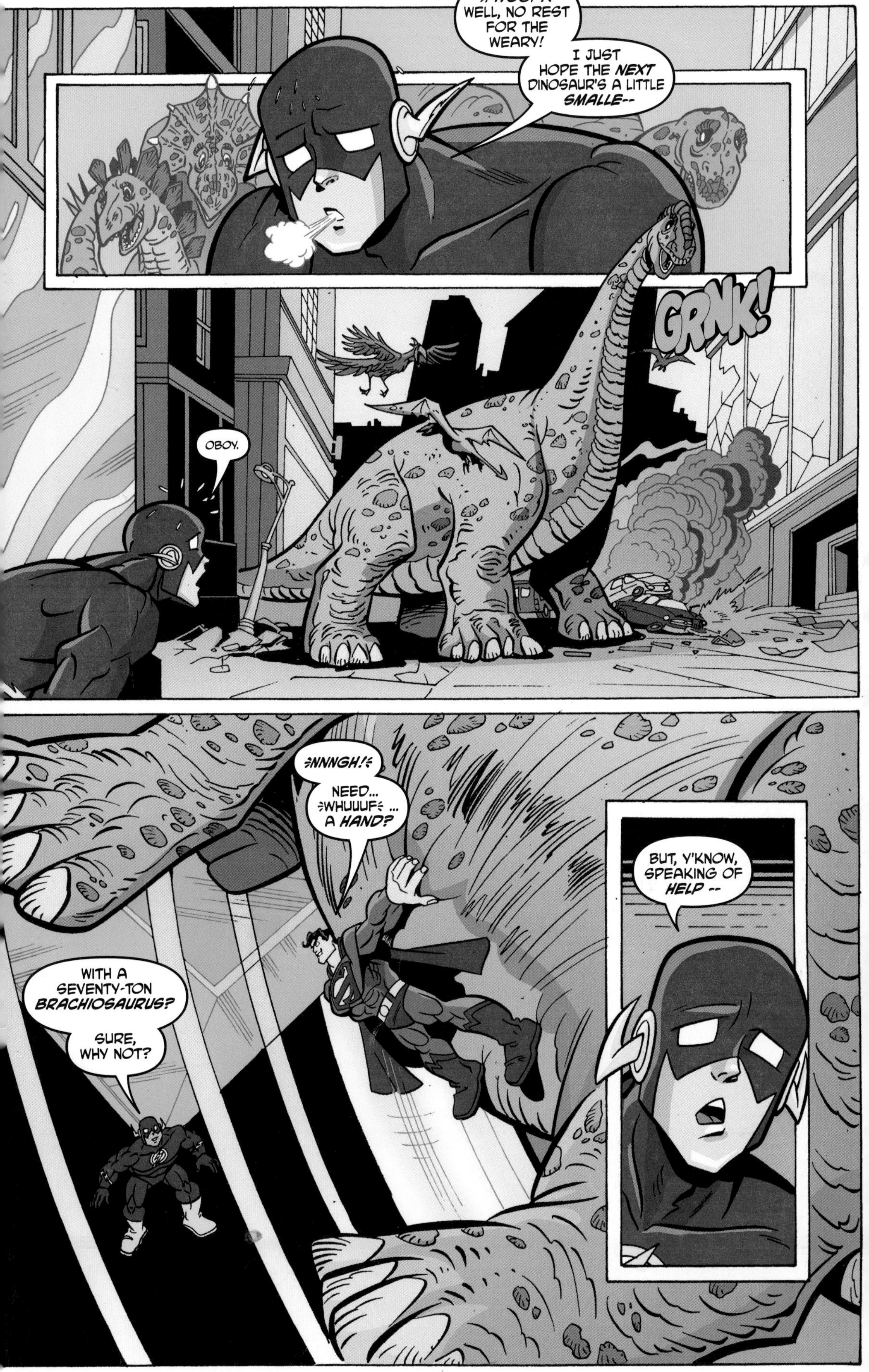

FWOOF! WELL, NO REST FOR THE WEARY!
I JUST HOPE THE NEXT DINOSAUR'S A LITTLE SMALLE--
GRNK!
OBOY.
NNNGH! NEED... WHUUUF ... A HAND?
WITH A SEVENTY-TON BRACHIOSAURUS?
SURE, WHY NOT?
BUT, Y'KNOW, SPEAKING OF HELP --

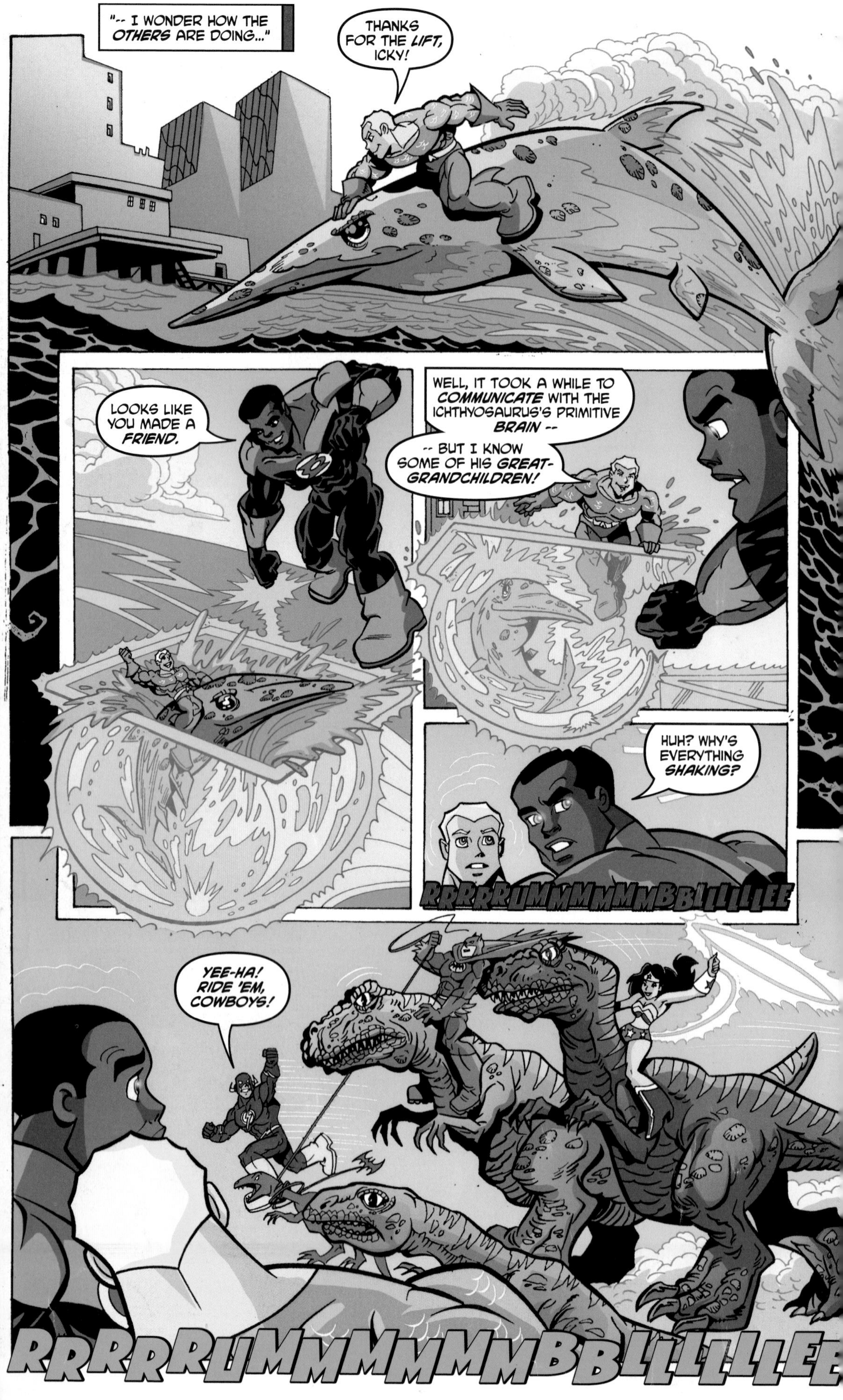
"-- I WONDER HOW THE OTHERS ARE DOING..."
THANKS FOR THE LIFT, ICKY!
LOOKS LIKE YOU MADE A FRIEND.
WELL, IT TOOK A WHILE TO COMMUNICATE WITH THE ICHTHYOSAURUS'S PRIMITIVE BRAIN --
-- BUT I KNOW SOME OF HIS GREAT-GRANDCHILDREN!
HUH? WHY'S EVERYTHING SHAKING?
RRRRRUMMMMMMMMBBLLLLLLEE
YEE-HA! RIDE 'EM, COWBOYS!
RRRRRUMMMMMMMMBBLLLLLLEE

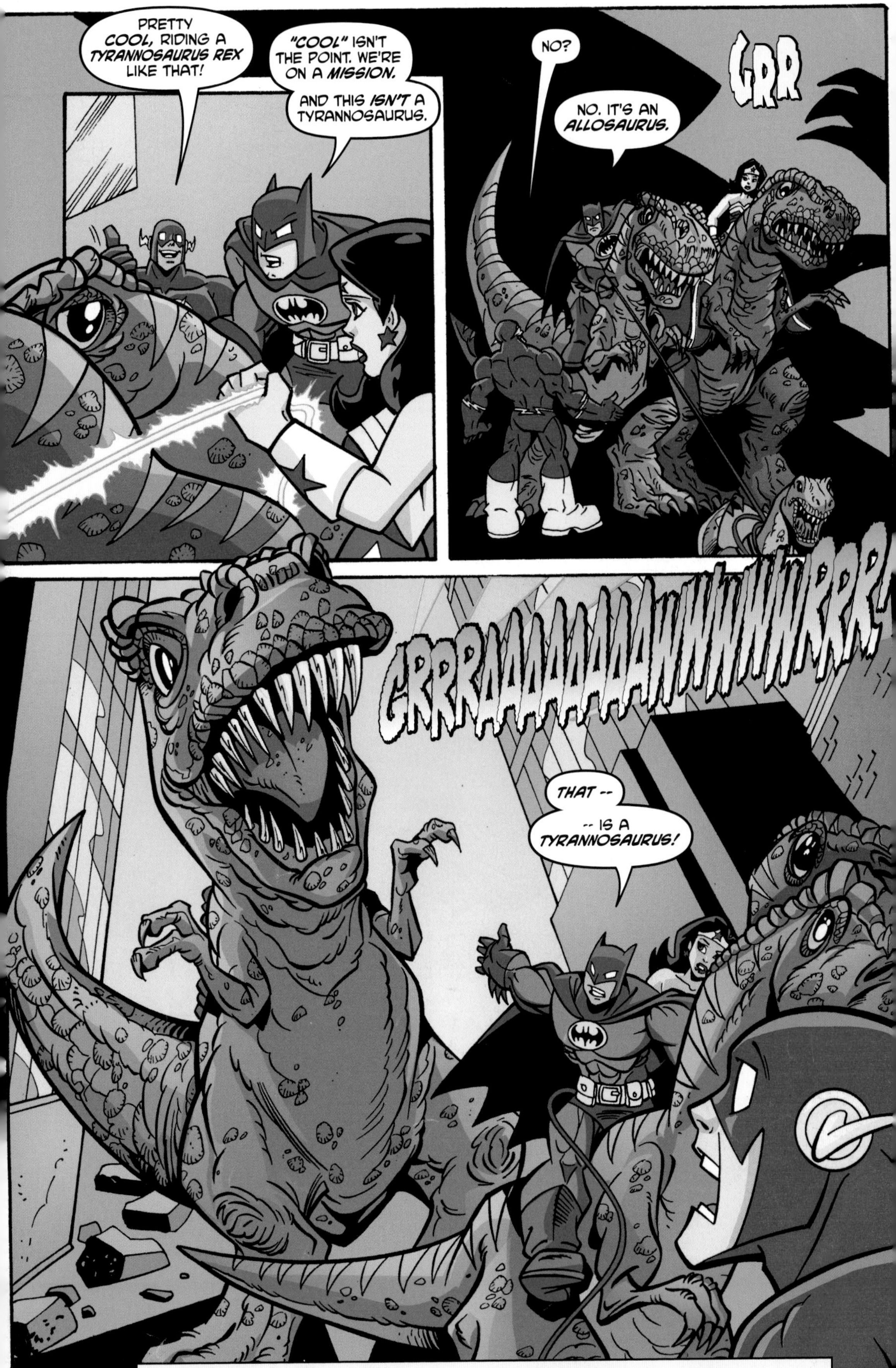

PRETTY COOL, RIDING A TYRANNOSAURUS REX LIKE THAT!
"COOL" ISN'T THE POINT. WE'RE ON A MISSION.
AND THIS ISN'T A TYRANNOSAURUS.
NO?
NO. IT'S AN ALLOSAURUS.
GRR
CRRRAAAAAAAAWWWWWRRR!
THAT --
-- IS A TYRANNOSAURUS!
YOU GUESSED IT -- THE OTHER DINOSAURS WERE JUST A WARM-UP! KEEP READING TO SEE THE SUPER FRIENDS TACKLE THE MOST FEARSOME DINOSAUR OF ALL IN CHAPTER 3!

DINOSAUR ROUND-UP
CHAPTER 3

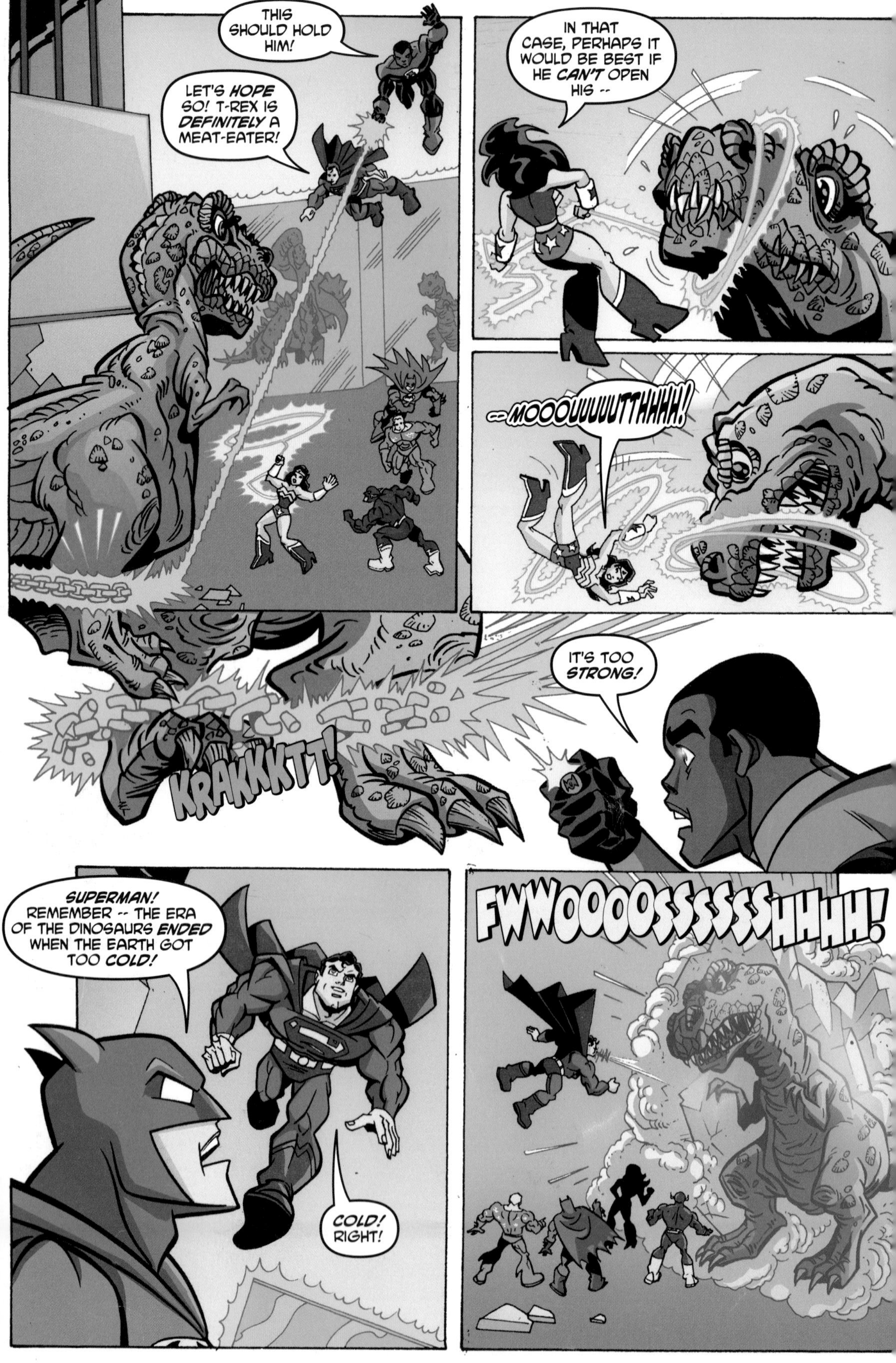
THIS SHOULD HOLD HIM!
LET'S HOPE SO! T-REX IS DEFINITELY A MEAT-EATER!
IN THAT CASE, PERHAPS IT WOULD BE BEST IF HE CAN'T OPEN HIS --
--MOOOUUUUUTHHHH!
IT'S TOO STRONG!
KRAKKKTT!
SUPERMAN! REMEMBER -- THE ERA OF THE DINOSAURS ENDED WHEN THE EARTH GOT TOO COLD!
COLD! RIGHT!
FWWOOOOOSSSSSSHHHH!

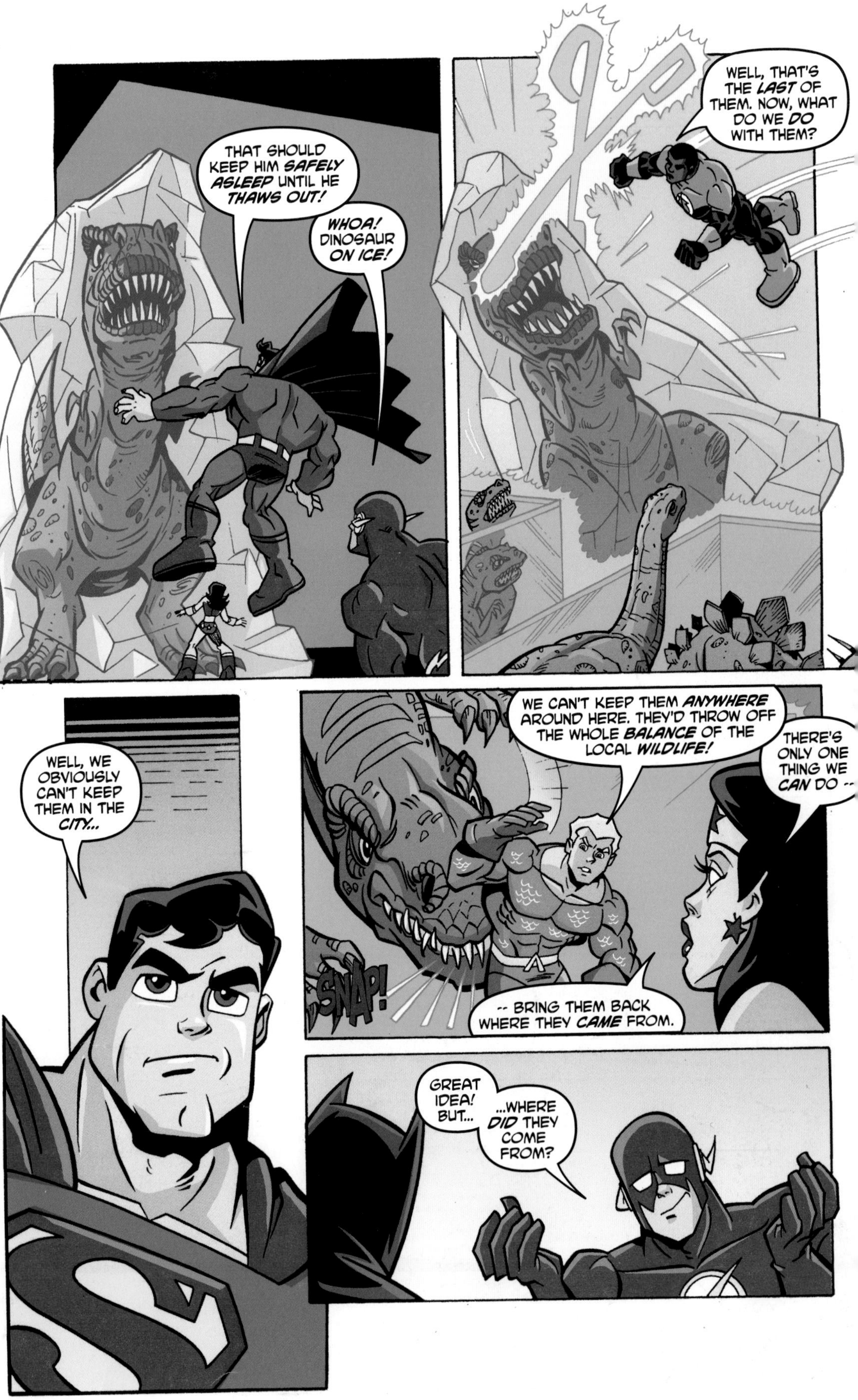
THAT SHOULD KEEP HIM SAFELY ASLEEP UNTIL HE THAWS OUT!
WHOA! DINOSAUR ON ICE!
WELL, THAT'S THE LAST OF THEM. NOW, WHAT DO WE DO WITH THEM?
WELL, WE OBVIOUSLY CAN'T KEEP THEM IN THE CITY...
WE CAN'T KEEP THEM ANYWHERE AROUND HERE. THEY'D THROW OFF THE WHOLE BALANCE OF THE LOCAL WILDLIFE!
THERE'S ONLY ONE THING WE CAN DO --
SNAP!
-- BRING THEM BACK WHERE THEY CAME FROM.
GREAT IDEA! BUT...
...WHERE DID THEY COME FROM?

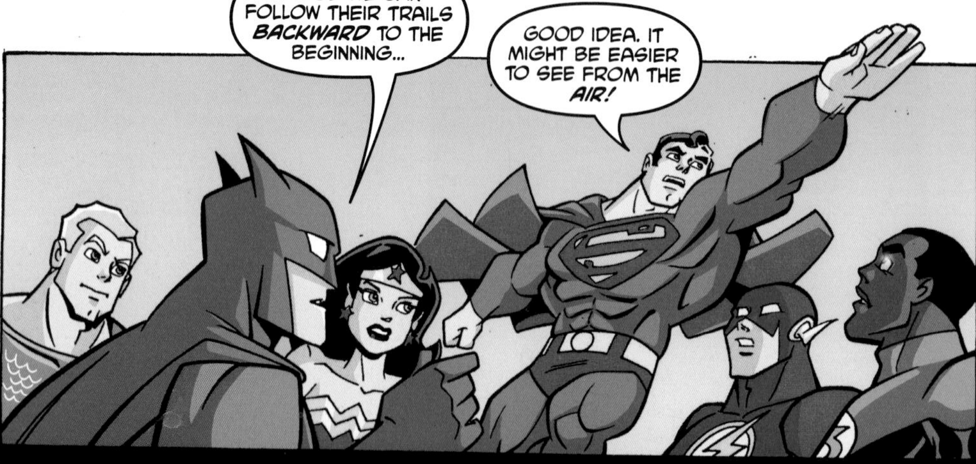
MAYBE WE CAN FOLLOW THEIR TRAILS BACKWARD TO THE BEGINNING...
GOOD IDEA. IT MIGHT BE EASIER TO SEE FROM THE AIR!

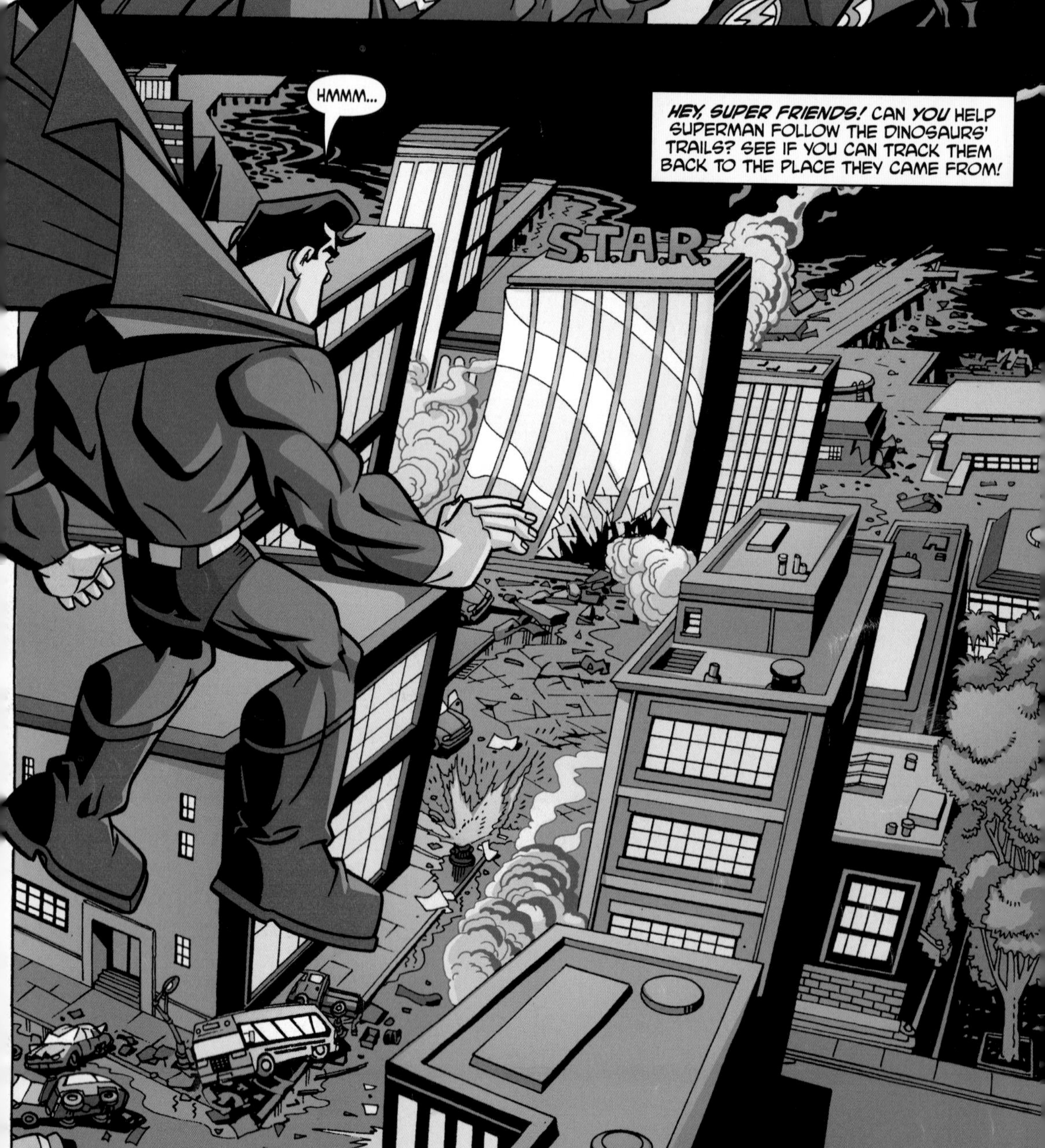
HMMM...
HEY, SUPER FRIENDS! CAN YOU HELP SUPERMAN FOLLOW THE DINOSAURS' TRAILS? SEE IF YOU CAN TRACK THEM BACK TO THE PLACE THEY CAME FROM!
S.T.A.R.

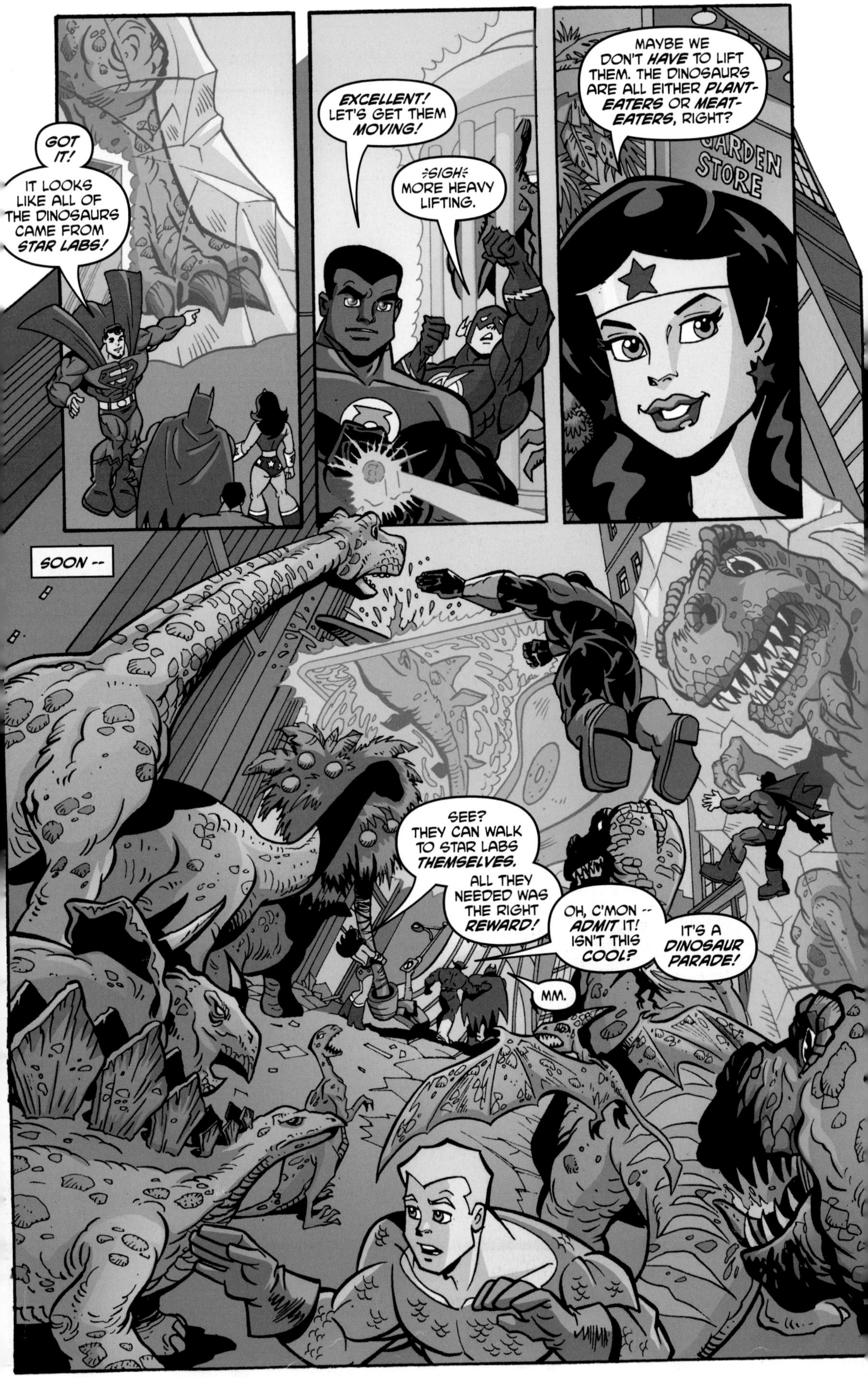
GOT IT!
IT LOOKS LIKE ALL OF THE DINOSAURS CAME FROM STAR LABS!
EXCELLENT! LET'S GET THEM MOVING!
SIGH MORE HEAVY LIFTING.
MAYBE WE DON'T HAVE TO LIFT THEM. THE DINOSAURS ARE ALL EITHER PLANT-EATERS OR MEAT-EATERS, RIGHT?
GARDEN STORE
SOON --
SEE? THEY CAN WALK TO STAR LABS THEMSELVES.
ALL THEY NEEDED WAS THE RIGHT REWARD!
OH, C'MON -- ADMIT IT! ISN'T THIS COOL?
IT'S A DINOSAUR PARADE!
MM.

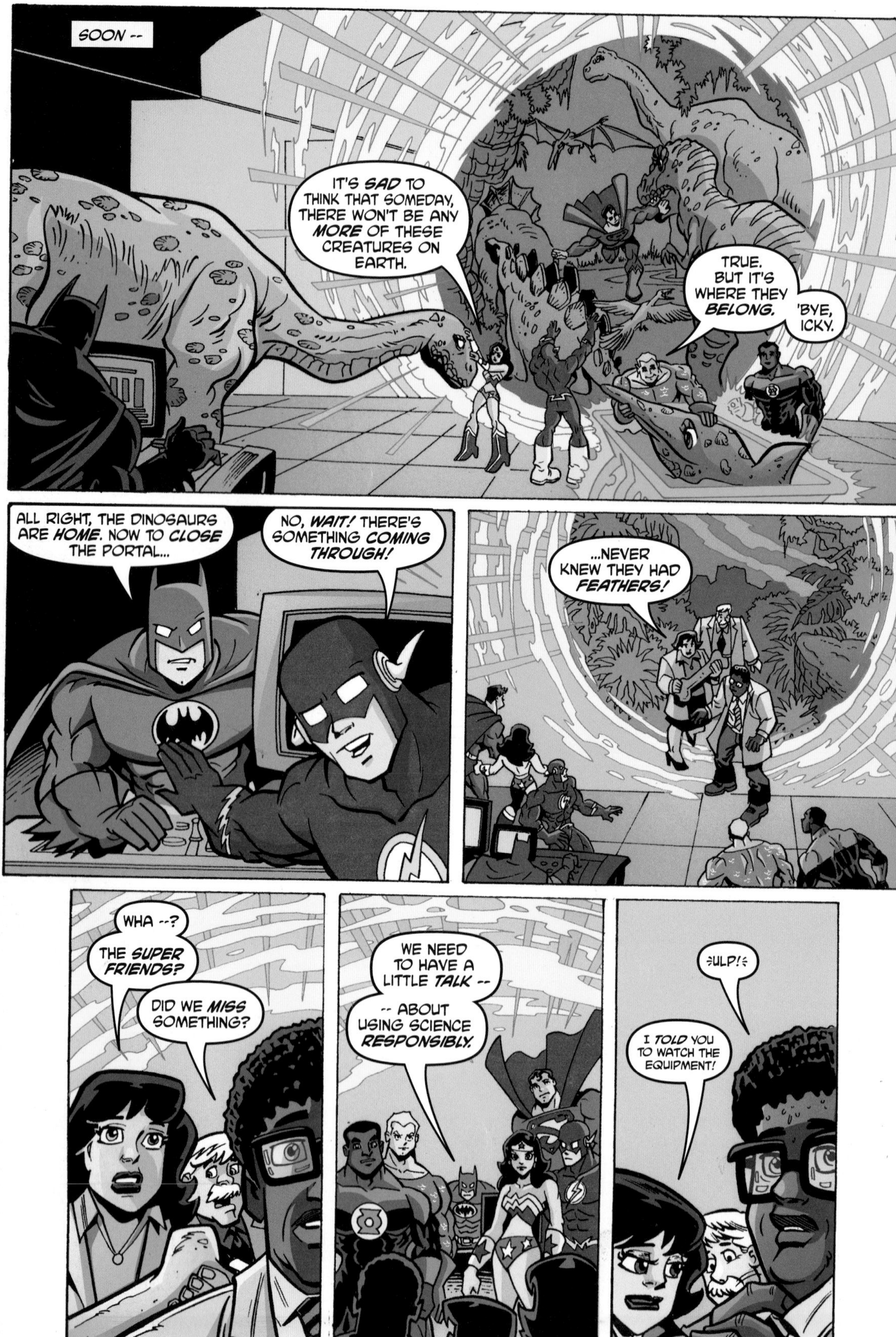
SOON --
IT'S SAD TO THINK THAT SOMEDAY, THERE WON'T BE ANY MORE OF THESE CREATURES ON EARTH.
TRUE. BUT IT'S WHERE THEY BELONG.
'BYE, ICKY.
ALL RIGHT, THE DINOSAURS ARE HOME. NOW TO CLOSE THE PORTAL...
NO, WAIT! THERE'S SOMETHING COMING THROUGH!
...NEVER KNEW THEY HAD FEATHERS!
WHA --?
THE SUPER FRIENDS?
DID WE MISS SOMETHING?
WE NEED TO HAVE A LITTLE TALK --
-- ABOUT USING SCIENCE RESPONSIBLY.
ULP!
I TOLD YOU TO WATCH THE EQUIPMENT!

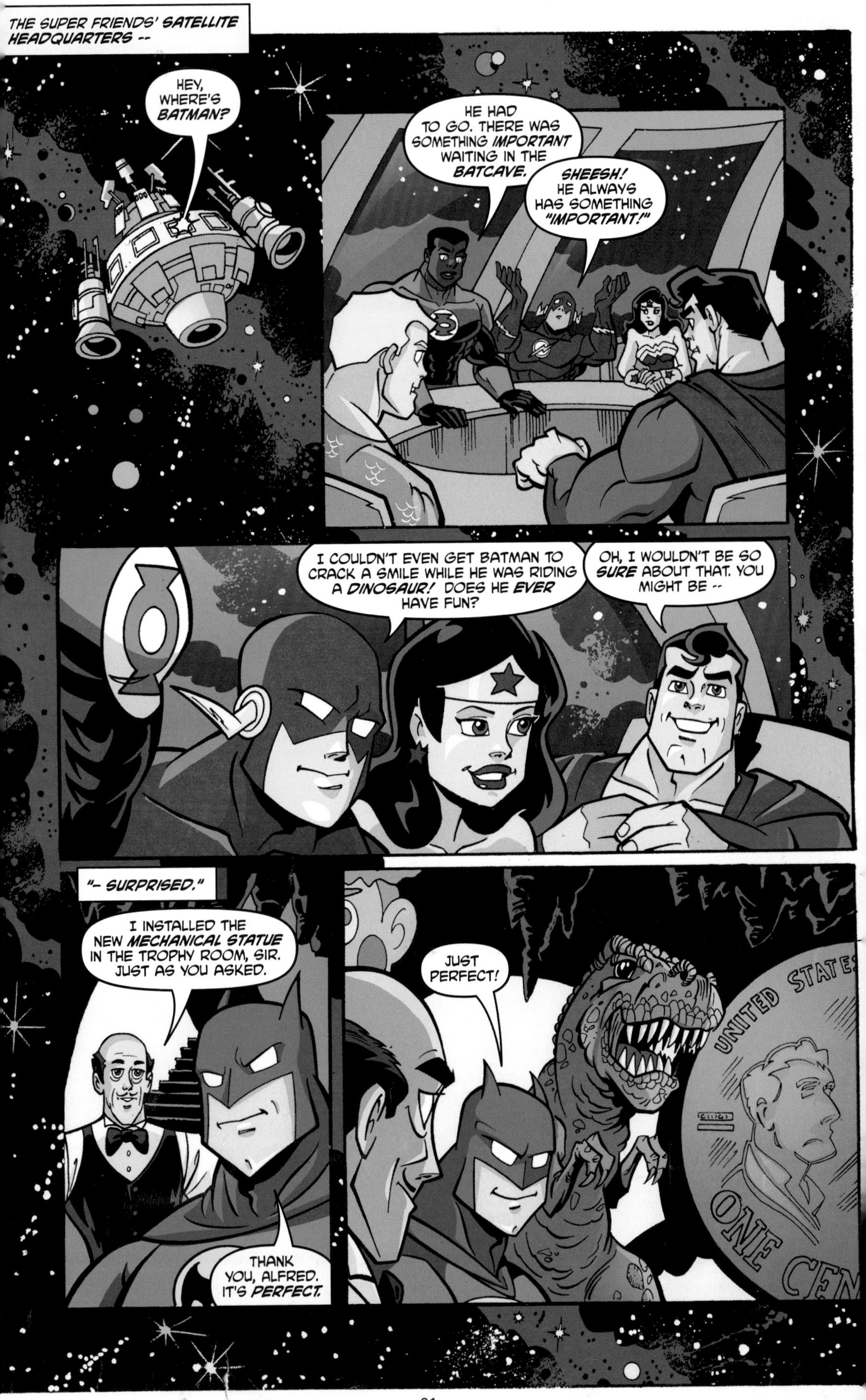
THE SUPER FRIENDS' SATELLITE HEADQUARTERS --
HEY, WHERE'S BATMAN?
HE HAD TO GO. THERE WAS SOMETHING IMPORTANT WAITING IN THE BATCAVE.
SHEESH! HE ALWAYS HAS SOMETHING "IMPORTANT!"
I COULDN'T EVEN GET BATMAN TO CRACK A SMILE WHILE HE WAS RIDING A DINOSAUR! DOES HE EVER HAVE FUN?
OH, I WOULDN'T BE SO SURE ABOUT THAT. YOU MIGHT BE --
"-- SURPRISED."
I INSTALLED THE NEW MECHANICAL STATUE IN THE TROPHY ROOM, SIR. JUST AS YOU ASKED.
THANK YOU, ALFRED. IT'S PERFECT.
JUST PERFECT!
UNITED STATES
ONE CEN

ATTENTION, ALL SUPER FRIENDS!

HERE'S THIS BOOK'S SECRET MESSAGE:

GSIN IOKDGBYU WBE MKX RB KXWINSXQ – OTOX IKDO RSXBP!

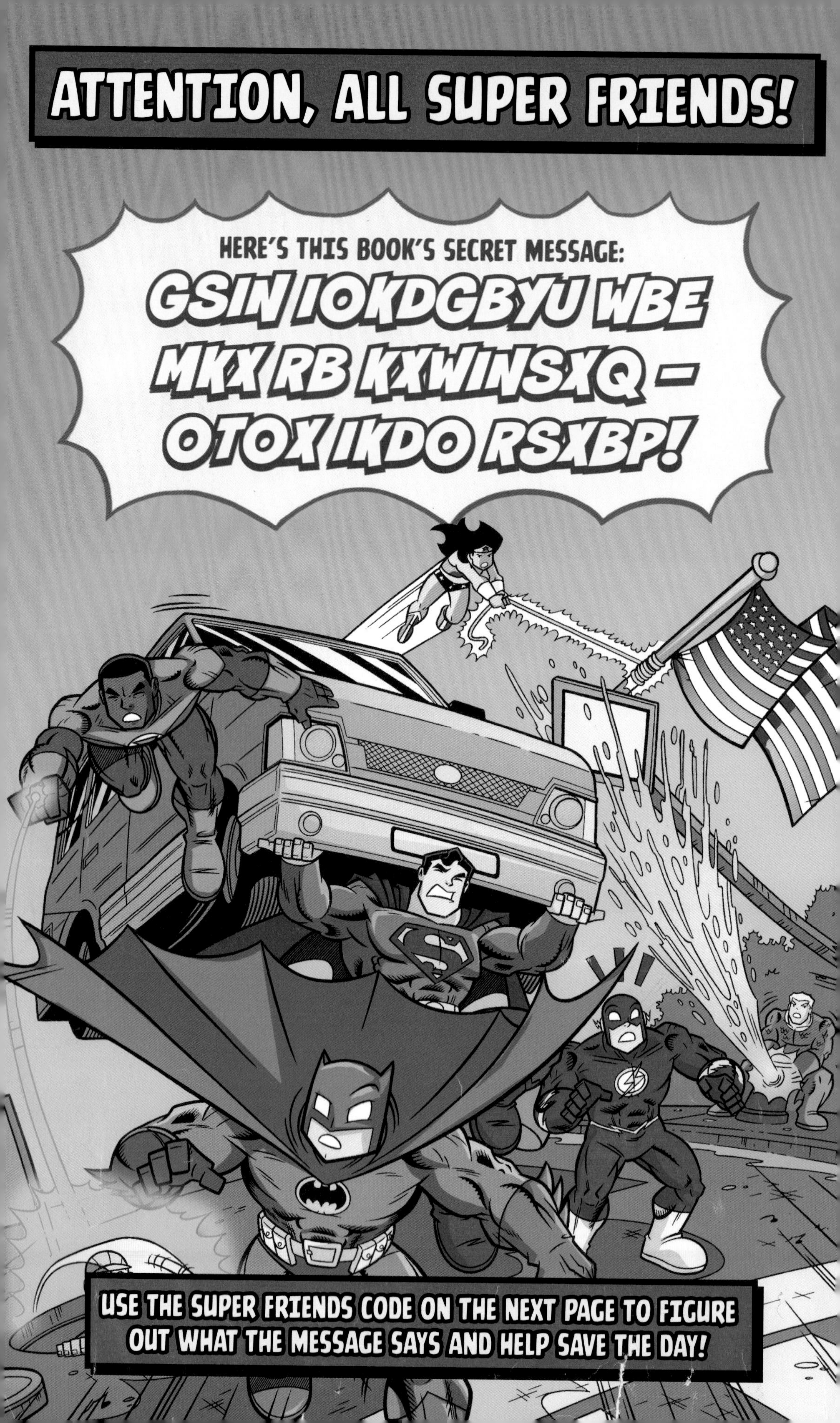

USE THE SUPER FRIENDS CODE ON THE NEXT PAGE TO FIGURE OUT WHAT THE MESSAGE SAYS AND HELP SAVE THE DAY!

HEY, SUPER FRIENDS! YOU CAN JOIN OUR TEAM--

--BY BEING A SUPER FRIEND!

BE KIND!

SHOW RESPECT!

HELP OUT!

DON'T FORGET TO USE THE CODE TO READ OUR SECRET MESSAGES IN EVERY ISSUE!

SUPER FRIENDS SECRET CODE
(KEEP THIS AWAY FROM SUPER-VILLAINS!)

A = Q	J = Z	S = I
B = O	K = A	T = V
C = F	L = X	U = K
D = M	M = C	V = P
E = U	N = H	W = Y
F = J	O = E	X = N
G = W	P = S	Y = R
H = B	Q = G	Z = L
I = T	R = D	

KNOW YOUR SUPER FRIENDS!

SUPERMAN

Real Name: Clark Kent

Powers: Super-strength, super-speed, flight, super-senses, heat vision, invulnerability, super-breath

Origin: Just before the planet Krypton exploded, baby Kal-El escaped in a rocket to Earth. On Earth, he was adopted by a kind couple named Jonathan and Martha Kent.

BATMAN

Secret Identity: Bruce Wayne

Abilities: World's greatest detective, acrobat, escape artist

Origin: Orphaned at a young age, young millionaire Bruce Wayne promised to keep all people safe from crime. After training for many years, he put on costume that would scare criminals - the costume of Batman.

WONDER WOMAN

Secret Identity: Princess Diana

Powers: Super-strong, faster than normal humans, uses her bracelets as shields and magic lasso to make people tell the truth

Origin: Diana is the Princess of Paradise Island, the hidden home of the Amazons. When Diana was a baby, the Greek gods gave her special powers.

GREEN LANTERN

Secret Identity: John Stewart

Powers: Through the strength of willpower, Green Lantern's power ring can create anything he imagines

Origin: Led by the Guardians of the Universe, the Green Lantern Corps is an outer-space police force that keeps the whole universe safe. The Guardians chose John to protect Earth as our planet's Green Lantern.

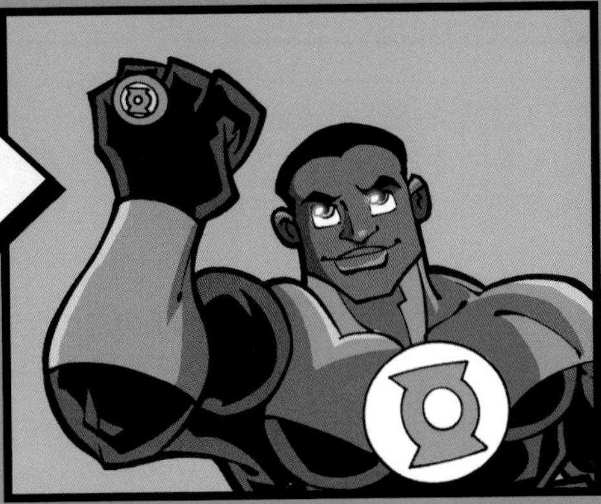

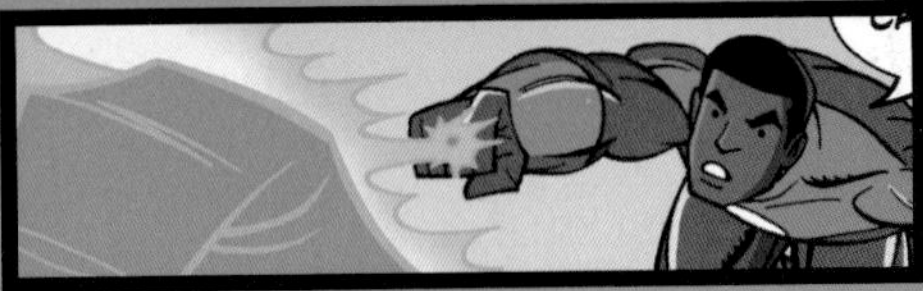

THE FLASH

Secret Identity: Wally West

Powers: Flash uses his super-speed in many ways: he can run across water or up the side of a building, spin around to make a tornado, or vibrate his body to walk right through a wall

Origin: As a boy, Wally West became the super-fast Kid Flash when lightning hit a rack of chemicals that spilled on him. Today, he helps others as the Flash.

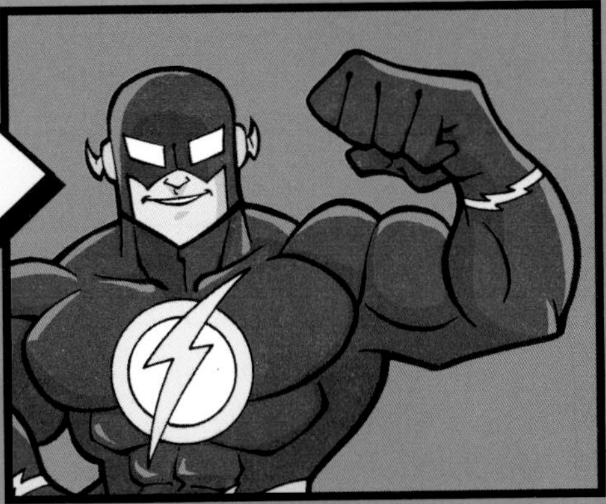

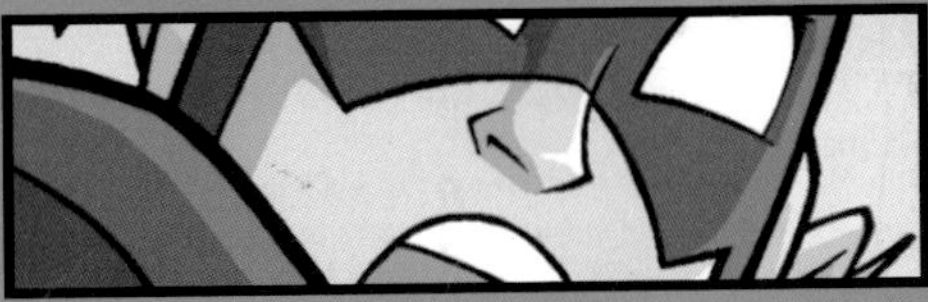

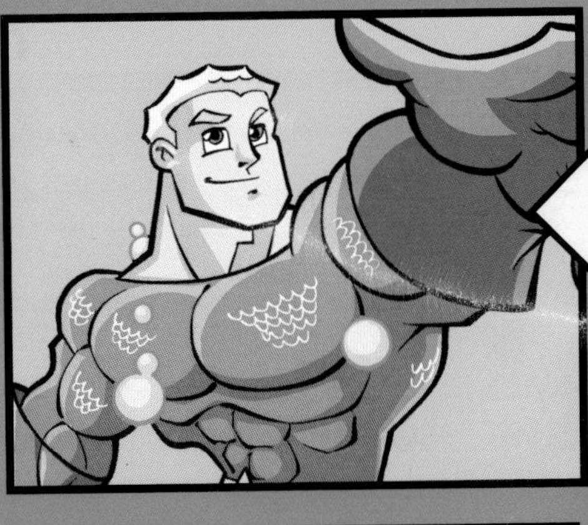

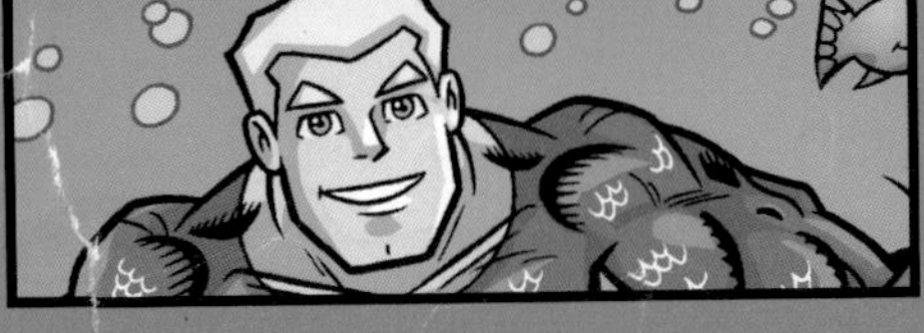

AQUAMAN

Real Name: King Orin or Arthur Curry

Powers: Breathes underwater, communicates with fish, swims at high speed, stronger than normal humans

Origin: Orin's father was a lighthouse keeper and his mother was a mermaid from the undersea land of Atlantis. As Orin grew up, he learned that he could live on land and underwater. He decided to use his powers to keep the seven seas safe as Aquaman.

CREATORS

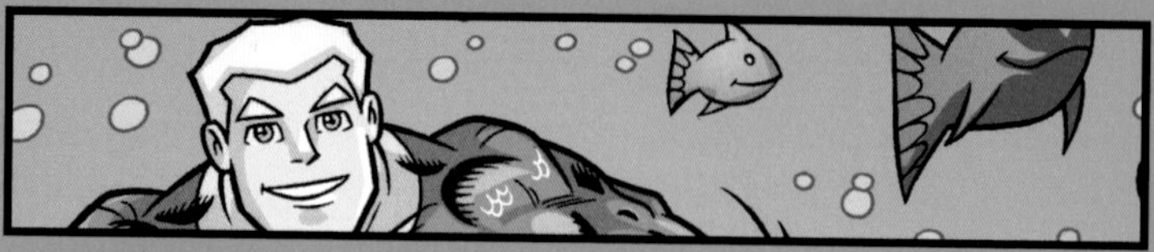

SHOLLY FISCH WRITER

Bitten by a radioactive typewriter, Sholly Fisch has spent the wee hours writing books, comics, TV scripts, and online material for more than 25 years. His comic book credits include more than 200 stories and features about characters such as Batman, Superman, Bugs Bunny, Daffy Duck, and Ben 10. Currently, he writes stories for Action Comics every month, plus stories for Looney Tunes and Scooby-Doo. By day, Sholly is a mild-mannered developmental psychologist who helps to create educational TV shows, web sites, and other media for kids.

JOE STATON ARTIST

Joe Staton has been a professional comic book writer and illustrator for more than 30 years. He's illustrated dozens of series for DC Comics and Marvel Comics, including Super Friends, Power Girl, and many more. Most recently, his work appears in the popular comic book series Scooby Doo: Where Are You?

HORACIO OTTOLINI ARTIST

Horacio Ottolini is a professional comic book artist whose works for DC Comics include Super Friends, Looney Tunes, Scooby-Doo, and many more.

J. BONE COVER ARTIST

J.Bone is a Toronto based illustrator and comic book artist. Besides DC Super Friends, he has worked on comic books such as Spiderman: Tangled Web, Mr. Gum, Gotham Girls, and Madman Adventures.

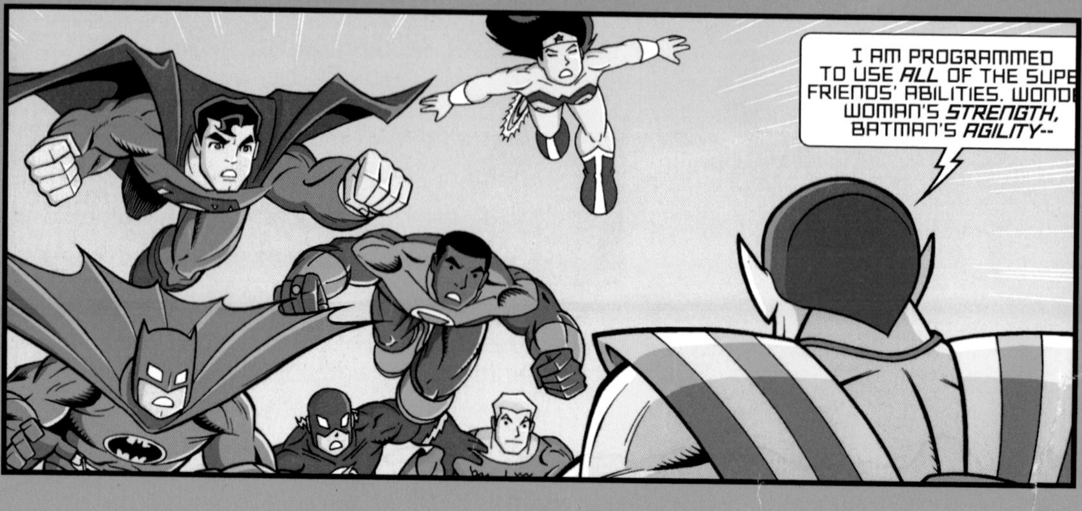
I AM PROGRAMMED TO USE *ALL* OF THE SUPE FRIENDS' ABILITIES. WOND WOMAN'S *STRENGTH,* BATMAN'S *AGILITY*--

GLOSSARY

allosaurus [AL·uh·sore·uhs]—a large, meat-eating dinosaur

armored [AR·murd]—covered with protective scales, spines, etc.

brachiosaurus [BRAY·kee·uh·sore·uhs]—a plant-eating dinosaur with a massive body and very long neck

communicate [kuh·MYOO·nuh·kate]—to share information, ideas, or feelings with another person by talking, writing, etc.

endangered species [en·DAYN·jurd SPEE·sheez]—a type of plant or animal that is in danger of becoming extinct

equipment [i·KWIP·muhnt]—the tools and machines needed for a particular purpose

harbor [HAR·bur]—a place where ships shelter or unload their cargo

ichthyosaurus [IK·thee·oh·sore·us]—a fishlike reptile from the Jurassic period

mechanical [muh·KAN·uh·kuhl]—operated by machines

mental [MEN·tuhl]—to do with or done by the mind

primitive [PRIM·uh·tiv]—very simple or crude

responsibly [ri·SPON·suh·blee]—done in a way that is sensible and trustworthy

satellite [SAT·uh·lite]—a spacecraft that is sent into orbit around the Earth, the moon, or another heavenly body

stegosaurus [STEG·uh·sore·uhs]—a plant-eating dinosaur with a small head; large, triangular plates along the back; and a heavy, spiked tail

tornado [tor·NAY·doh]—a violent, whirling column of air that appears as a dark cloud shaped like a funnel. A tornado travels rapidly and usually destroys everything in its narrow path.

tyrannosaurus rex [tie·RAN·uh·sore·uhs REX]—a large meat-eating dinosaur that walked on two legs

vegetarians [vej·uh·TER·ee·uhns]—people who eat only plants and plant products and sometimes eggs or dairy products

VISUAL QUESTIONS & PROMPTS

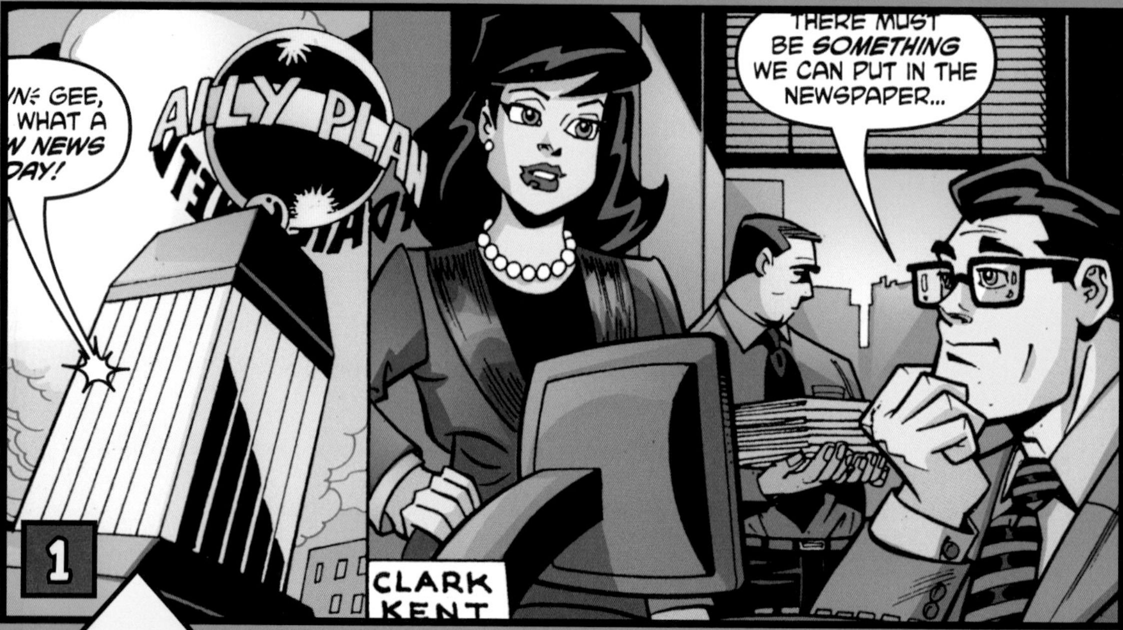

GEE,
WHAT A
NEWS
DAY!
CLARK
KENT
THERE MUST BE *SOMETHING* WE CAN PUT IN THE NEWSPAPER...

1. Look at the building in the left part of the panel above. What is this building? Who works there? How do you know?

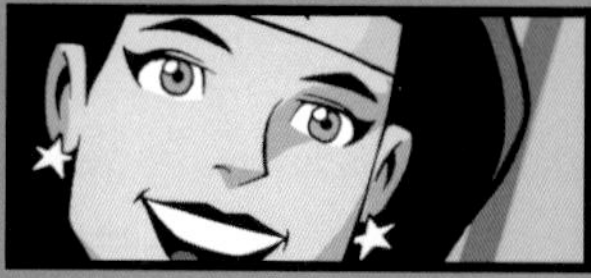

2. Even though some of the dinosaurs are vegetarians, they were not considered harmless. Why not? What specific examples are given in the art?

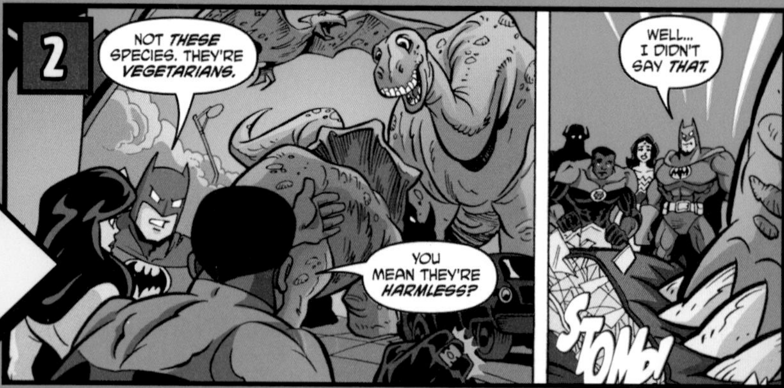

NOT *THESE* SPECIES. THEY'RE *VEGETARIANS.*
YOU MEAN THEY'RE *HARMLESS?*
WELL... I DIDN'T SAY *THAT.*
STOMP!

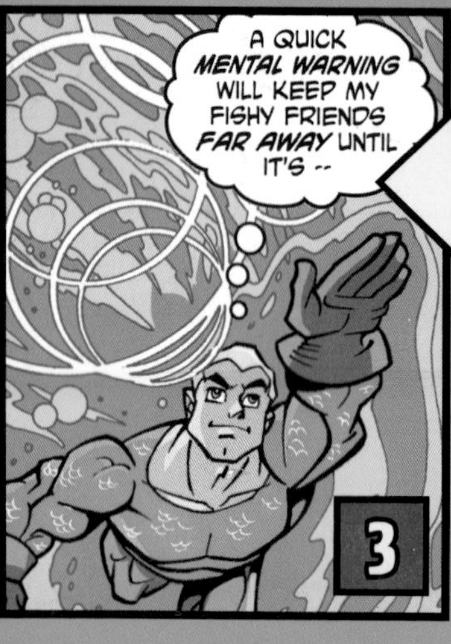

A QUICK *MENTAL WARNING* WILL KEEP MY FISHY FRIENDS *FAR AWAY* UNTIL IT'S --

3. Aquaman is sending a mental warning to the fish in the sea in the panel at left. What visual clue are we given of this mental warning?

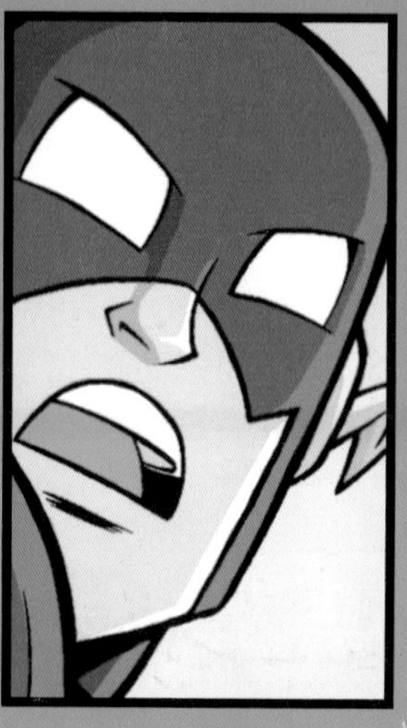

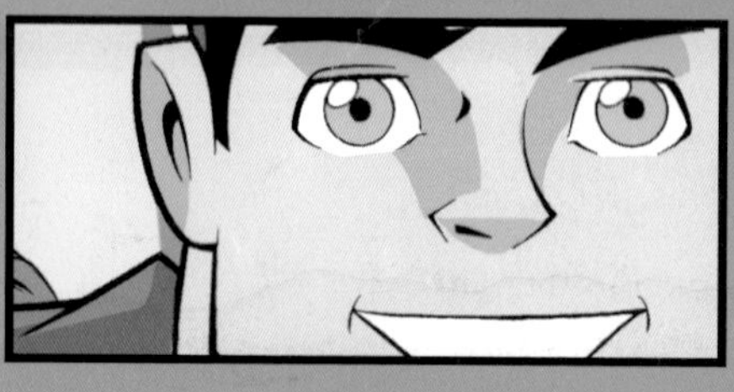

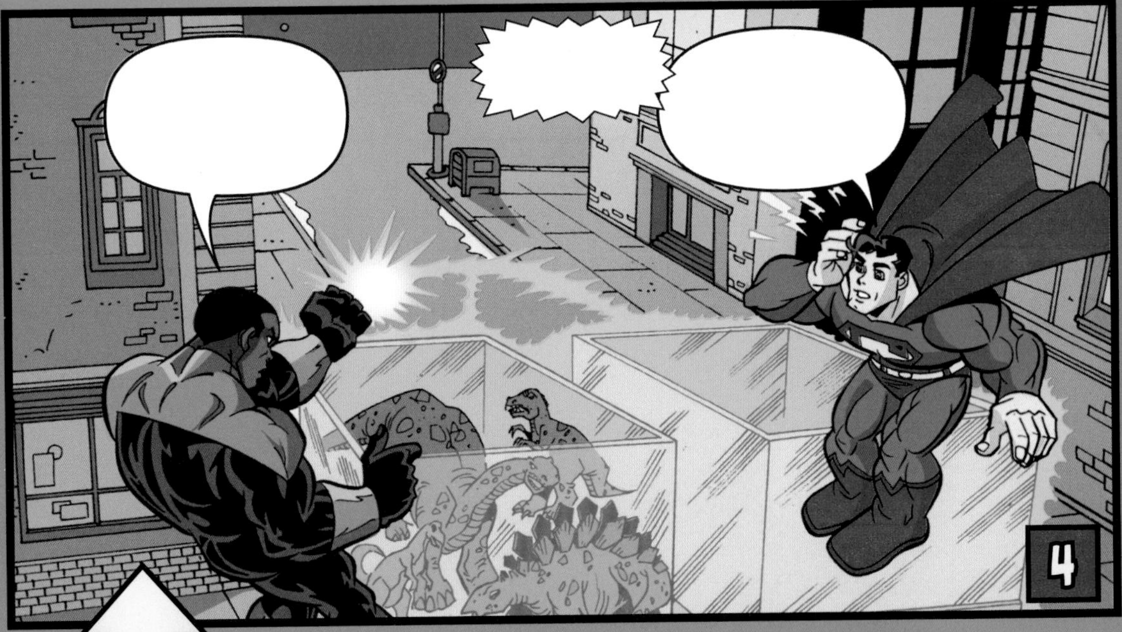
4

4. Pretend you are a comic book author, and write the dialogue for the scene above.

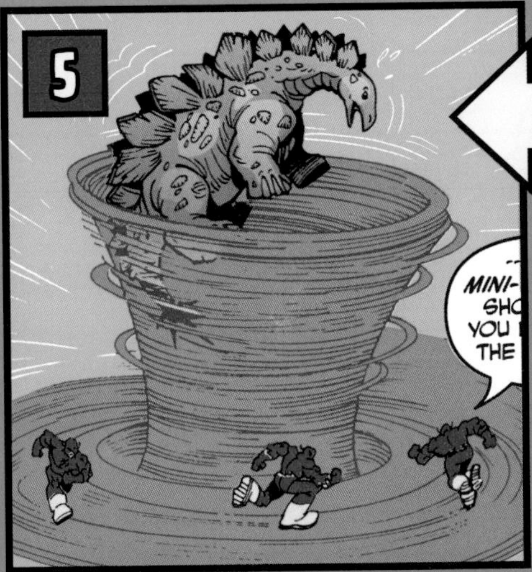
5
MINI-

5. When the artist wants to show Flash in movement, there are often three or more Flash characters shown in the same panel. Why do you think the artist chose to do this? What does this effect mean?

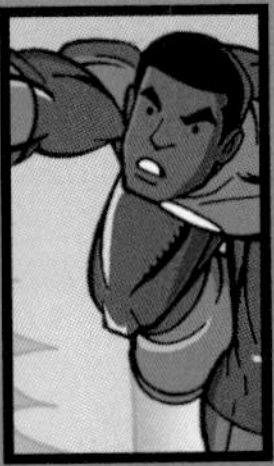

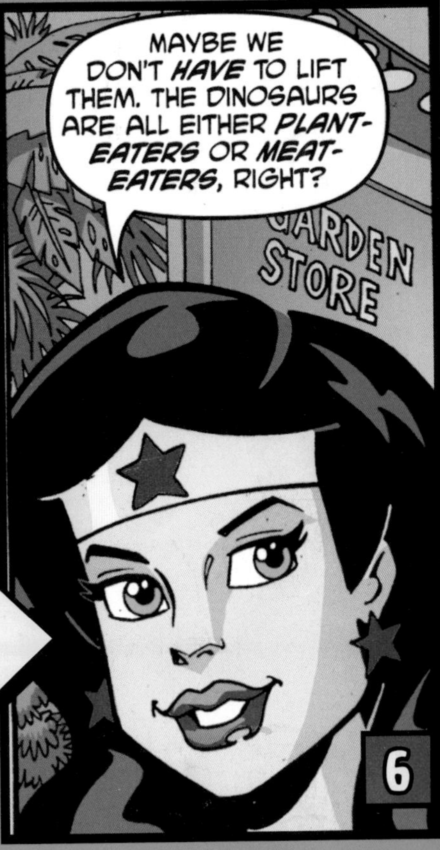
MAYBE WE DON'T *HAVE* TO LIFT THEM. THE DINOSAURS ARE ALL EITHER *PLANT-EATERS* OR *MEAT-EATERS*, RIGHT?
GARDEN STORE
6

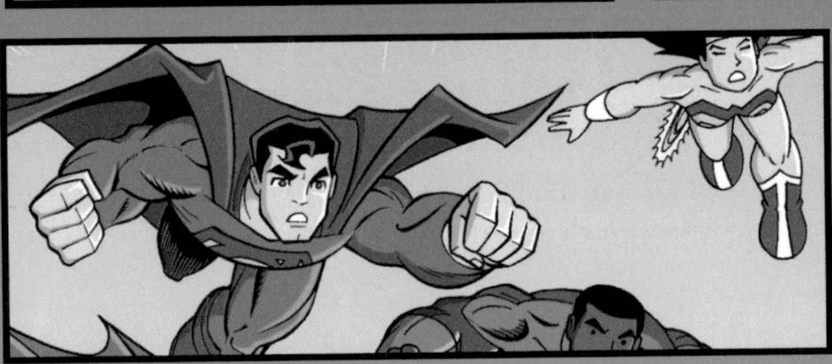

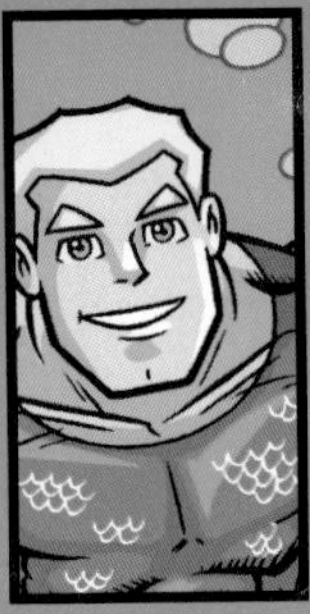

6. Wonder Woman has a plan to use bait to get the dinosaurs to follow the Super Friends. The panel at right shows us a clue about her plan. What is the clue? What does she use as bait?

READ THEM ALL!

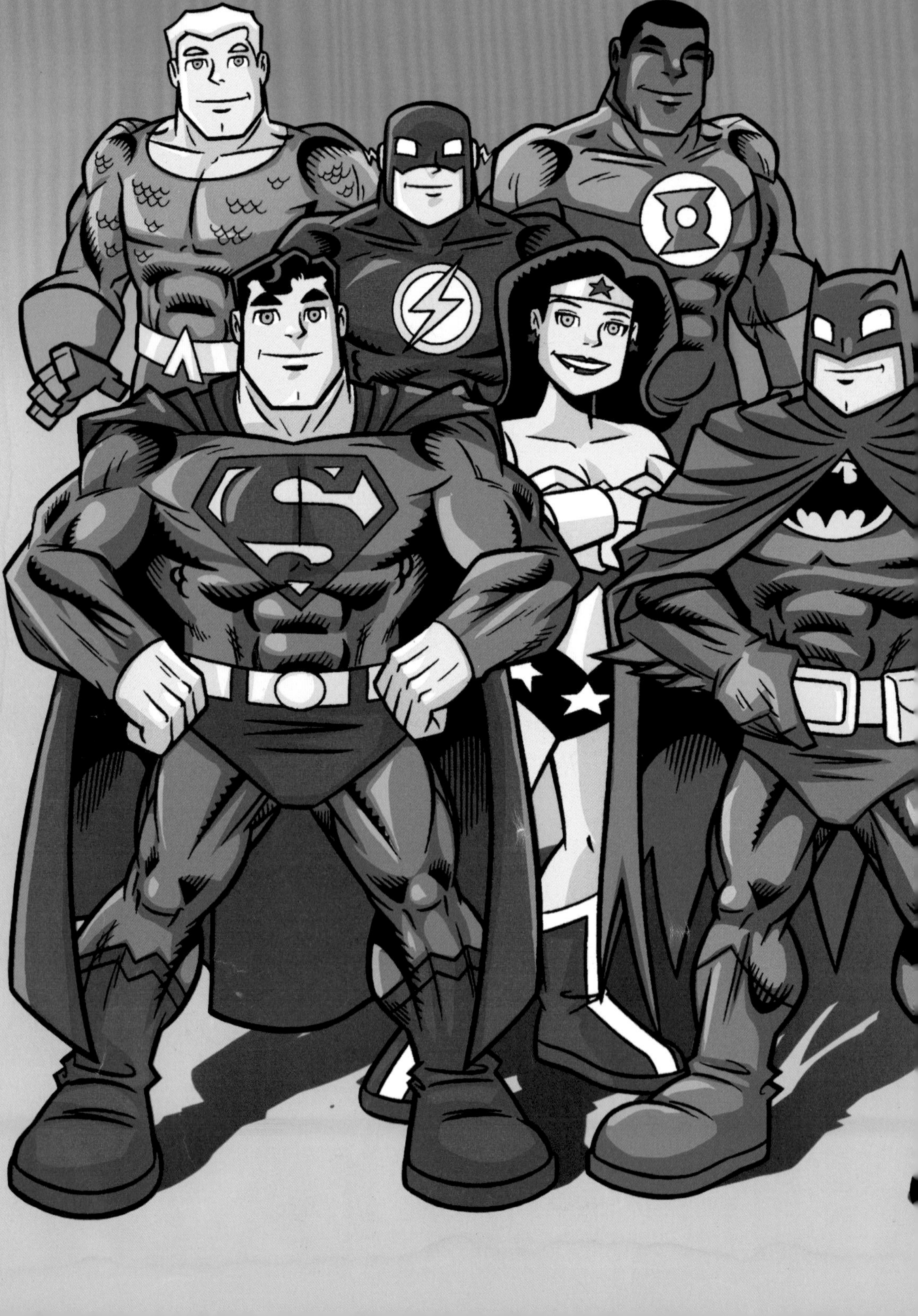

DC SUPER FRIENDS™

DC COMICS
DC SUPER FRIENDS
HUNGRY FOR POWER
Fisch • Brizuela
Hungry for Power

DC COMICS
DC SUPER FRIENDS
DINOSAUR ROUND-UP
Fisch • Ottolini • Staton
Dinosaur Round-up

DC COMICS
DC SUPER FRIENDS
WANTED: THE SUPER FRIENDS
Fisch • McKenny • Moy
Wanted: The Super Friends

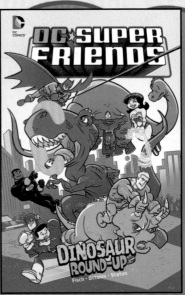

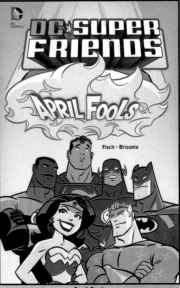

DC COMICS
DC SUPER FRIENDS
APRIL FOOLS
Fisch • Brizuela
April Fools

ONLY FROM...

STONE ARCH BOOKS™
a capstone imprint www.capstonepub.com

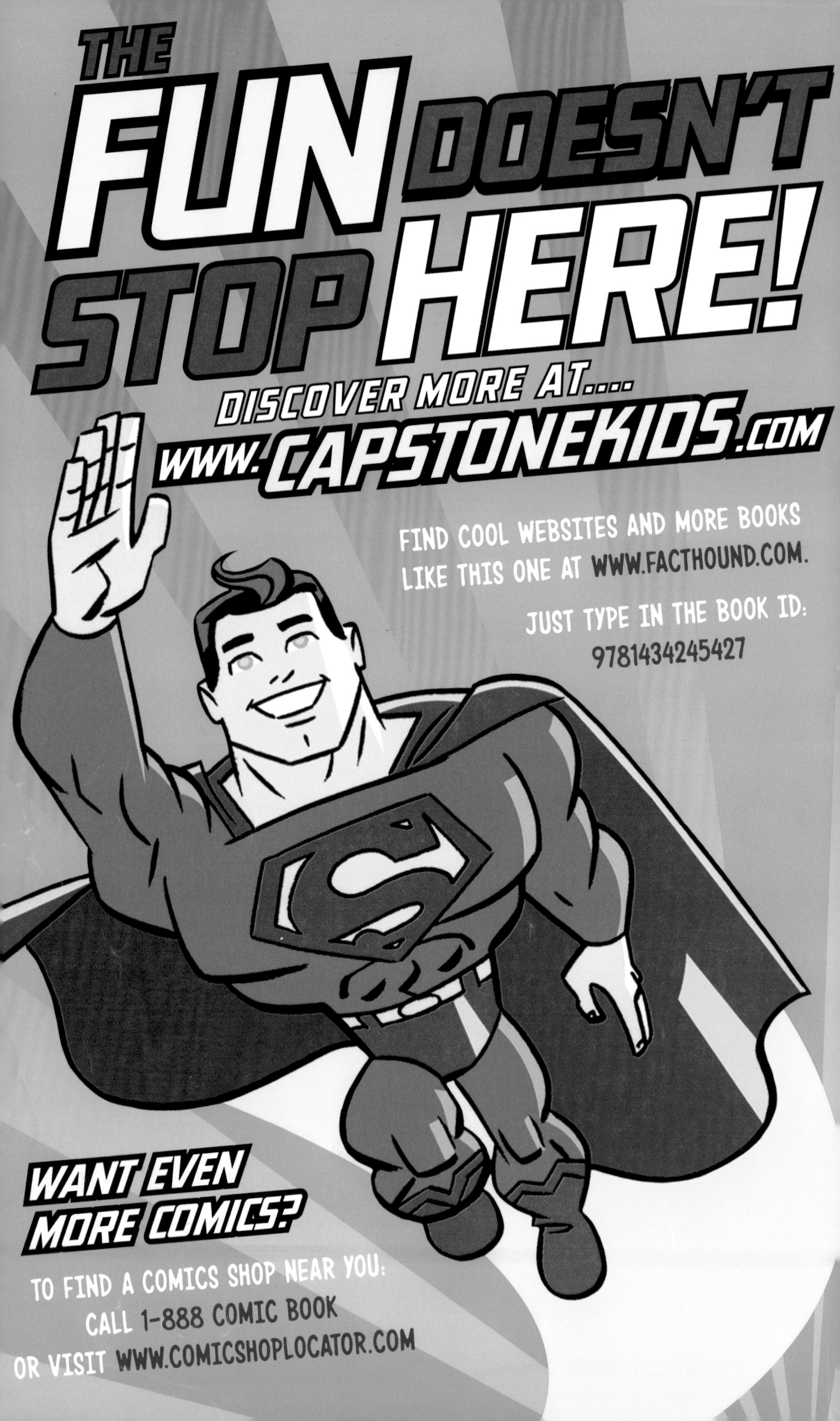
THE FUN DOESN'T STOP HERE!
DISCOVER MORE AT....
WWW.CAPSTONEKIDS.COM
FIND COOL WEBSITES AND MORE BOOKS LIKE THIS ONE AT WWW.FACTHOUND.COM.
JUST TYPE IN THE BOOK ID: 9781434245427
WANT EVEN MORE COMICS?
TO FIND A COMICS SHOP NEAR YOU:
CALL 1-888 COMIC BOOK
OR VISIT WWW.COMICSHOPLOCATOR.COM